LAST JUNCTION

By
Connor de Bruler

MONTAG

A Montag Press Book
www.montagpress.com
Montag Press
777 Morton Street, Unit B
San Francisco CA 94129 USA

Montag Press, the burning book with the hatchet cover, the skewed word mark and the portrayal of the long-suffering fireman mascot are trademarks of Montag Press.

Printed & Digitally Originated in the United States of America
10 9 8 7 6 5 4 3 2 1

"Best of luck to those with dark talents,
and no good fortune."

— Roberto Bolaño

1

Their first kiss had been in the confession box of a derelict chapel. After that night, he would never see her again. She had shared not only the company of the same sleeping bag and a can of Vienna sausage, but secrets, secret knowledge yet to be recorded in books; old stories from her native Montana, stories of plains and dead chiefs and forgotten places where other travelers had formed cities. She had a bottle of Popov and had given him a few deep pulls. He swallowed the burning mouthfuls and made love slow while the pit bull slept in the nave between the rotted wood of the pews. Nights like those kept him going as he went from place to place, easing the boredom and loneliness of his endless wander.

Rayne had chosen to become a crust punk, embracing the American traveler's code, tagging his way across rail cars, bumming cigarettes from open-minded bystanders, subsisting off garbage bins and soup kitchen meal, in the same way, he imagined, the children of the Mongolian steppe might decide to become monks. What got him to this decision was a storm of failure through life and school: undiagnosed dyslexia, drunk papa Dorn's six rules for living under the same roof, and a tattered copy of Kerouac's *Desolation Angels*: the only possession of his mother's

that Dorn had not immolated in the backyard pit at one point or
another with his Seneca brand cigarettes and a bottle of lighter
fluid squeezed over the many articles of clothing and scraps of
documentation as if it were mustard.

"Some folks just get locked in shitty lives," Dorn had told him
once, "Tattoo *that* on your forehead, fuckin' faggot."

When Rayne finally took off, two days before his seventeenth
birthday and four before he lost track of the calendar, he knew what
he left would be burned out back, his posters, blankets, non-gutter
punk clothing; all gone in the flames. But his record collection...
that was something Dorn couldn't have. He took the milk-crate,
filled to the brim with vinyls, and stashed it beneath the bridge
where he had chalked his first tag, thinking it better to let some kid
find it, someone who would care--a last act of charity.

For a long time the road didn't have teeth. Winding strips of
asphalt and endless unraveling spools of railroad track flowed like
a river carrying him to places he had not even seen in dreams:
Purple Fiddle, Asheville, Omaha, Eugene. There were other des-
tinations without signs, or people; places where he felt safe, where
he slept on the grass. He ate blueberries beneath moss-encrusted
aqueducts in a forest, and never really knew what state he was in,
the time of day, or where he was headed next. He would lie on a
rock beside a stream and watch deer graze on the opposite bank
in morning fog. He met a couple in Ohio with a gas stove and a
malamute who shared their coffee and toasted bread with him.
An old guy in Texas bought him eggs Florentine at a diner, then
asked him for a blowjob. The old guy tried to handcuff him to
a tractor trailer, but Rayne stabbed him with his apple knife. He
had to use it again on the highway in Nebraska.

Eugene, Oregon was Bodh Gaya, Bihar, India for the punk
crowd. Every traveler made the pilgrimage once a year or so,

treading softly on hallowed ground—a strict religious adherence to flippancy and buck-shot-grade honest conduct in their eternal search for booze and dope. A crust punk would caveat asking a straight for a dollar by telling them what it was for: heroin, crack, cheap beer, cigs. But when they asked for a handout for something useful, there was an unspoken trust that only straights from the West Coast bought into. Stationary people back east didn't give a damn. Rayne befriended a shirtless guy who called himself Cuba. He had a couple tallboy cans of Watermelon Steel Reserve.

"Yeah, so, it's bum wine. The kind of shit they sell to under-age black kids. Make it taste like Kool-Aid, get'em hooked. They got mango blunt wraps now."

The sun was setting on the town. Cuba pointed to the train depot.

"Let's go sit in that brick arch there like old-school bums and get more fucked up."

Rayne looked up at the crow's nest and saw another nomad setting up his squat for the night. He had a German shepherd by his side and started cleaning his fingernails with a blade.

He parted ways with Cuba when he found out none of the other punks wanted him around. He had broken some code, but no one would tell Rayne just what had happened since it was guilt by association. After that, he didn't head north to Washington like the rest of them. Instead, he hopped the train somewhere dry and wandered around a downtown that looked like it was built to disorient alcoholics like lab mice. He ran into a girl sitting on the ground between a bar and a bicycle shop. She had a *Replacements* shirt and a couple Andre the Giant is my posse and Misfits patches on her hat, flying a flag that read "Dog killed on rail car. Need booze to forget." Dogs were a good way to keep safe, but

Rayne never liked the idea of being responsible for another creature's needs on the road. He walked up to her and asked which state they were in.

"I don't fuckin' know. Buy a map."

A college-looking prep walked up to her with a four pack of tallboys, dangling the cans over her.

"Pull off two," he said.

"That's what I'm fuckin' talking about," she said, as she took the beers and stashed them in her bag.

Rayne turned to the college guy, who he imagined had raped someone at least once, and asked him which state he was in.

"The state of confusion, my nigga," he said.

Rayne was white and so was the prep who disappeared into a crowd of similarly dressed white kids. He tried to read the Greek scratching across their uniform sweatshirts but saw nothing to indicate where he was. The desert, he guessed.

The girl looked back up at him.

"The fuck you still here for?"

Rayne walked off into the dust.

That's when the road grew teeth.

2

When you are young and homeless, people try not to see you standing out in the cold, try to make you invisible, unaware it was them you were trying to erase, imagining the world whispering to you in the silence of a deserted city empty of other's thoughts.

Unlike God, the world spoke. It spoke in the trees and lakes and wind and dust, a topographical language of chance and dark tides. At times, rain fell like urine from a drunk's bladder and other days the terrain was as dry as the cracked lips of an unwanted assaulter's kiss.

It wasn't long after he had jumped his most dangerous train yet—he couldn't count the rotating lug nuts—that he landed somewhere in the Southeast.

Nowhere close to a depot, the train had stopped in a town square beside a sports arena, a row of houses, and the remnants of a quarry. He walked through the fog once the rain stopped. On the train, he found a place on the edge of the V-car, knee deep in gravel with a flimsy sheet of industrial rubber above his head and pack in a heavy downpour. He watched the pines roll by in the semi-black of the young night.

Now, he followed the red neon glare and the scent of jellied greases up the damp sidewalk to the fast-food dumpster where he found a couple of wrapped, still-good sandwiches. He took them up the hill fortified by rotted beams and ate one of them. A cat came crawling out of the fern and hissed at him. He tossed it half a sandwich. It wouldn't eat it till he was gone, so he left prematurely, having thought it might have been a good spot to catch a doze.

He wandered through a college neighborhood with more ferns and some palm plants. There were narrow streets of cobbled gray brick. He had seen an empty tennis complex with a clubhouse that he couldn't get inside, and stepped past a courtyard adorned with armless Romanesque statues and well-manicured hedges. Someone had strung up speakers to play the sound of trickling water, but there was no actual source to be found. The eccentricity and uselessness of it terrified him.

He imagined he was now in Florida, but had no evidence other than the palms. He found a grotto in a little college park and slept there for the night.

3

By morning, the campus police had slapped him with a vagrancy charge and driven him out to what looked to be the local skid row. At least now he knew where he was: Columbia, South Carolina. He figured he'd take the next Maersk freighter north. The security was tighter on the name brand lines, but they barreled through at a steadier pace. If you could muster the courage to evade the bulls, you could get to where you were going ten times faster. Bulls, he thought. The term had come out of the Great Depression for rail car security and stuck ever since. He had heard it first in a literature class in some old short story, and couldn't imagine that the modern train riders still used it. He was wrong. Feeling the courage from getting busted once already that day, he took his chances and scaled the end of a flatcar carrying a Hanjin container. It was a standing trip the whole way, but he was moving at the pace of lightning. The train glided over gravel beneath the city and later through an estuarine swamp with egrets and Muscovy ducks nested in the shallow slime among the lily pads. That was what he got to see more than anything--day-long expanses of uninterrupted natural terrain, like he was hiding inside of a screen saver. Then again, as he thought about it, these many vistas in his memory couldn't have been as unsullied as he had first perceived them, since there was a million ton loco-motive that bellowed noxious gas through all of them.

The swamp evaporated into pines and, slowly, the pines changed to poplar and oak and grew a thick coat of kudzu. Once the kudzu turned to rocks he knew he was in North Carolina or Tennessee again. It didn't matter which state or where. He fig-ured one day after his travels had ended, he'd get out a map, or some kind of electronic hologram, because who knew what kind of technology the future had, and he would be able to see all of the miles he had gone and all the towns he had visited.

The rain fell hard. He was significantly colder up this way. He took his jacket out of his pack and headed out of the rail yard and made his way through the evergreens and massive oaks. He passed through a field with a derelict barn and eventually found a road. The sign pointed in two directions, one way to the inter-state, the other to town. He walked down the grassy shoulder of the road surrounded by trees. When the sky was overcast, night fell quick and he was having trouble seeing. The trees turned to shadows and the rain became a sensation rather than something he could see in the air. The weather picked up and he was forced to drape himself in the hazmat poncho he had sewn out of an old tarpaulin Dorn had used to cover his busted Camaro. It kept him dry, but it was cumbersome to walk in. The material was dark too, hard for people to see in the night, which, at least half the time, was a good thing. All he could hear was the chatter of the rain hitting the tarp.

He remembered his mother and her favorite book: *Desolation Angels*. He had not taken the book with him when he left (you can't say you ran away if no one is chasing you). He couldn't remember everything about it, having only read a few pages. He liked listening to his mother talk about it more than he had ever enjoyed the book itself. She had said something to him about Kerouac playing an imaginary game of baseball in his head at the foot of the mountain lookout. He had fantasized about being a loner in the forest and only hallucinating mundane things because his daily life was that much out of the ordinary. His current surroundings suggested he had pretty much accomplished just that. But he still didn't see the ghost of Jack Kerouac fucking his mother. Instead, he had a secret Vietnam in his head. There were enemy soldiers mobilizing through the shadowland beyond the road. He had to move like a ghost to keep from their reach.

In the distance a pair of headlights flickered to life. He could hear the soft crunch of tire tread and smell the scent of exhaust as the silhouette of a tall vehicle rolled up behind him. The SUV took up half the asphalt. He stepped ever further to the right, hugging the trunk of a damp tree, to let the driver pass, but the driver stopped. He kept walking again and the SUV's tires crawled, inch by inch, behind him. Knowing that he was being followed, he jumped to the opposite side, ran through a dense thicket of evergreens and rhododendrons, slid down a shallow embankment before falling into the dense cushion of his pack, and did what he could to blend in with the earth. Behind him, a single beam, not from the SUV, but from a high-powered flashlight, oscillated over the terrain where he lay, hiding. A bull wouldn't be looking for him this far from the yard. That was impossible.

He could see the rain falling in the lens of the flashlight. There were two or three moments when he thought the driver had spotted his face, when he primed his legs to keep running, but instead the near-disembodied beam of what reminded him of a grim institutional austerity kept scanning the forest. The man finally lowered his flashlight in a common stance that suggested he was giving up, but, in a breathless second, took his first leap into the woods after him. The makeshift poncho he was under was too loud in the rain. He wriggled out of it like snake hide and slid further down the embankment, sidestepping to the covered refuge of a languishing rhododendron. He flipped open the fruit sampling blade: a long, thin piece of steel with a little dried blood from the man in Nebraska. By then, the driver of the SUV, whose features were still hidden in the dark, knelt down and inspected his tarpaulin poncho with the light. Rayne took the opportunity to run past him—amid the noise of the downpour on the crinkling material—up the embankment and back to the fog-covered road where the SUV sat, locked and parked on the shoulder. He studied the side of the vehicle, nothing stood out, nothing that said police. There was no insignia from the cargo company. It was just a car.

He tried to get a look inside the slate-colored windows when a pair of eyes looked back, bulging egg-whites with azure retinas and dark-matter pupils cutting through the lightlessness as if they were worlds all their own. They belonged to the grim smiling face of a child, head askew, looking back at him through the window tint, still as a corpse. His adrenaline ran fast enough to feel as though it were crystallizing in his joints, damming up his veins, when he realized that it was no child in the passenger's seat but an intricate doll with a painted face and small flannel clothing. The doll stared back, nutcracker mouth barely agape as it sat alone in the vehicle. He hid in the trees above the SUV as the driver got back to the road. The figure had the poncho balled up in his arm and set it in the back seat. The doll's face appeared to follow him even as the car drove away.

He shivered in his jacket and watched the last flicker of the taillight's glare in the distance. He was getting soaked without the poncho. Why had the bastard taken it? He took off his cap to smooth back his unwashed hair, then tightened the bill down over his eyes. He crawled out of the woods and kept going down the road.

The town was bigger than he had imagined, but clustered together like a fortress which was not something he saw too often on the east coast; it was the way its main road sloped down into a treeless valley and suddenly broke into a steep climb toward a curtain of unnatural light. Midnight in the conservatory, alone with paint, like the meat of a true genius. He cut through a car lot and sat down in the shelter of an open doorway with a narrow stairwell. He rested on the bottom step, his feet on the cracked tile floor. There was a brass mail compartment on the left. It looked like something lifted from a museum. He dried off and let himself think. He saw a guy with an umbrella across the lot and immediately recognized his clothing. The punk wasn't flying a flag, but he was carrying a paper bag under his arm from the corner store. He waved him down in a fever of hope. The guy came over to the doorway on the edge of the sidewalk. He was older and had braids in his beard. Half his head was shaved to expose the union jack tattoo in his skull. He looked like a Viking.

"Sup, bro? You travelin'?"

"Yeah, I'm travelin'. Just got into town. Where is this?"

"This is Last Junction, North Carolina. Las Juncus! Best kept secret of the hills, man. You fixin' to get dry?"

"Fuck yeah."

"Well, follow me to the pass, brosef. We got us a fire barrel raging and Baltimora on loop."

He wasn't sure what anything he had said meant, but he followed the tall guy anyway.

"Where you from, man?"

"Nowhere important," Rayne said. "I was born overseas."

"You army?"

"Naw, my mom just came over for some guy. I lived a few different places. Mostly just Shitkickersville, Ohio."

"Where were you born?"

He asked him a question instead.

"Where are you from, man?"

"Chi-raq brother. Southside, Chicago. Only white kid in a ten block radius. But I've been in Virginia and around for some years now. Been all over too. Ridin'. It chooses you, pilgrim."

"That's for sure. You been to England?"

"Yeah, man. Been to London and Bristol," he said, tapping the union jack in his skull. "I got a back piece of the Michigan lakes too. You inked? I don't see much on you."

"I'm just starting out travelin'."

"You'll get you some stick-and-poll tats soon enough. Thing about tats is they're like railcar tags. Places you wanna remember get etched into your DNA or at least your epidermis."

He spoke like he was trying to sound smart. It might have been his way of trying to sound poetic. That was the one thing that crust punks were all adamant about--they wanted everyone to know they had the capacity to be financial analysts and college professors. A lot of the conversations devolved into intellectual pissing contests. He had in fact met some intelligent people along the way, but there had been too few. In their defense, stupidity and mental illness were hard to differentiate on the road. Perhaps stupidity was a form of mental illness. Of course, he had to hand it to the man for the hopeful advice. To think that one day he would ever see someplace or have an experience that he wanted to wear on his skin was of the same ilk of romanticism that got him on rails in the first place. So far, the only moments of his life he wore on his skin were bruises.

"What's your name?" Rayne said.

"I go by Crews. With and 'e' and a 'w' instead of a 'z'."

"My name's Rayne. With a 'y' and an 'e' on the end."

"That's a badass title, bro."

"Thanks."

"Is that the name you were born with?"

"No."

"What's your real name?"

"That kid's gone. Leave the past up to the past."

"Like you killed your other personality. That's cool," Crews said. "Unless you got warrants out for you."

"No, no warrants," he said, striding over a puddle. "Although, I got a fine down in South Carolina today for sleeping on a college campus."

"Yeah, we've been there. I knew this motherfucker outta Houston who kept his tickets in a scrapbook with all of his Polaroid photos. That was some funny shit."

They headed away from the main drag and hiked through a lumber yard. He saw flickering orange light on the opposite end of the yard beneath an iron bridge.

"Is that it?"

"Yeah, man," Crews said, lighting up a half-cigarette. He took a drag then passed it to Rayne. Rayne took the butt and gave it a quick inhale.

"Phew, menthol," he said exhaling.

"Beggars can't be choosers."

They arrived under the bridge in the warmth of the fire where six other gutter punks called after Crews as he passed around tallboy cans of Olde English and PBR. There was a girl in the far corner watching the rain, taking intermittent hits on a blackened crack pipe. One of the guys had a salvaged tape deck, playing an 80s song he had once heard in passing on the low setting. Rayne watched the girl in the corner cool off the pipe then stash it into a special collar. She walked over to Crews who gave her a beer and she sat down in the dirt.

Crews introduced Rayne to the group. There was no beer for him. He set his pack on the ground and took a seat in the reeds close to the rain-swollen creek.

A kid with a Slipknot sweatshirt yelled out to him, "How long you been here?"

"A couple minutes really."

"You got lucky we sent Crews out them, huh?"

"Yeah."

The kid hopped down to the bank of the river like an Orangutan and approached him. He grabbed hold of his pack and tinkered with the Velcro and buckles.

"You ain't been riding the rails too long have you? You got nice things."

"No, not too long."

"Hmm, seems odd to me. You sure you're a traveler?"

"Yeah, man."

Another kid with a facial tattoo laying his head on a girls lap with a can of Olde English on his stomach started berating the kid standing over Rayne.

"Leave'em alone, Golem!" he said and turned to Rayne. "We call this asshole Golem."

Golem turned to the kid on the slope.

"Hey, man. I'm trying to keep us protected."

Crews looked back at them.

"Rayne ain't gonna do nothing. He's good people."

"You don't know that shit, he just showed up like two seconds ago, bitch!"

"Shut up, Golem!"

"Yeah, shut up Golem!"

A girl threw an old beer bottle at him.

"If you could take your fuckin' hands off my shit, I'd appreciate it," Rayne said.

The kid skulked away and returned to drinking his beer.

Rayne clutched his pack tightly and attempted to relax and drift to sleep in the reeds, listening to the calming noise of the water.

4

The morning slammed into him like a cheap-wine hangover. Cold and shivering with fatigued muscles from never having gotten any true rest, he suffered a pressure in his chest he didn't understand coupled with a sudden, searing pain in his neck. Eyes wide open, he saw the Golem kid kneeling over him with a filet blade, trying to carve open his Adam's apple.

He caught the kid's hand and halted the knife. His attacker pressed down using gravity to drive the steel edge toward his throat.

Rayne diverted its path into the dirt, then pulled at Golem's eyelashes, trying to rip off the lid.

The kid took his knee off Rayne's chest as he retreated, shielding his eye.

"Fuckin' bitch."

Rayne could see his free hand was still holding the dirt-covered knife. He looked around for the others, hoping to elicit some kind of help, but they had all abandoned the underpass. The fire barrel smoldered in the gray of the overcast dawn. He looked around for his pack but didn't see it. Golem smirked as he primed the blade for a stabbing maneuver.

"They're gone," he said. "I chucked your shit in the river, dumbass. Too bad too. People would know who I jacked it from if I kept it."

Rayne picked up a clod of concrete and threw it at his face. The desperate effort was surprisingly effective. Golem's lip burst apart and blood began to dribble down his chin. He lunged at Rayne with the knife. Rayne side swept him at the final second and had him on the ground. He took out his own blade and stuck the long end into the kid's ear canal. When he tried to pull it out, he broke off the handle. He crawled away through the grass.

The kid stood on his knees, his mouth agape, breathing almost inaudibly. With his empty hands he grazed the broken wedge of the blade sticking from his ear.

"What did you do?"

"I stuck a knife in your head, asshole."

He picked up the same piece of concrete he had thrown at his attacker.

Tears streamed down the kid's face. Snot bubbled in his nostril.

"You have to take me to a hospital. Please, call someone. Call 911."

Rayne said nothing and knocked out his front teeth with the concrete. He dragged him by the hood of his sweatshirt into the shallow end of the creek. He held his face under until he felt sick with himself, then tried to pull him out, but he was already dead.

5

As far as he knew, Jack Kerouac had never killed anyone. He may have pulled a gun on a man in a San Francisco barroom, an admittedly ugly example of homophobia, but he had never taken someone's life, unlike his drinking buddy Billy S. Burroughs. But even Burroughs had just made a mistake, a drunken error, when he shot his wife in the skull instead of the glass balancing above it. As for any other writer he had previously admired, Rayne had always assumed there were a couple of unmarked graves in the Mojave Desert left there by Hunter S. Thompson for some old Hell's Angels members.

His path had unfortunately veered away from the writer's. Perhaps it was better this way since in reality he couldn't write a lucid sentence, even on adderall. He was an outlaw now. A volunteer of manslaughter. A man who could defend himself with deadly force. He was in closer company with Neal Cassidy, Billy the Kid and Carl Gugasian.

He had first panicked with the body and dragged it away from the creek bank, propping him up against the iron pillar of the bridge. There was a used syringe by the fire barrel. He stuck it in the kids arm, but quickly realized the facial bruises and knocked-out teeth were too obvious. Making sure the needle was jammed in an actual vein and not just the muscle of his thin elbow's crook, he kicked the body into the stream and followed it as it bashed into rocks and drifted into the greater river. Along the current, he spotted his pack wedged between two boulders. Now, he hadn't lost anything. It felt awful. He retrieved his pack and followed the body until it disappeared into a drainage culvert. His aim was for it to look like a random junkie had overdosed and drowned. Hitting the rocks would account for the blows and missing teeth. He thought about who might find the body, feeling horrible about himself. The first thing he needed to do was get the hell out of Last Junction.

He sat under an oak tree as the rain picked up. He touched his neck and looked at the semi-coagulated blood on his finger-tips. There was a long, superficial slash healing across his neck. All he could think about was the red line on his throat incriminating him. He didn't even know the kid's real name. It was strange to him, the more he thought, or the more clear his thoughts became as the paranoia settled and he was free to question events, that everyone had left the underpass so early without having rustled him awake. Where they in on it? All eight of them? It was unlikely. But they had flickered out of existence like spirits.

It was a long way to the railyard, longer than he remembered. He got a third of the way into town and saw the stairwell alcove he had rested in the night before. A man in a winter jacket was taking mail out of the brass slot. His breath was as thick as cigarette smoke. Rayne breathed on his hands under the eave of a brick building facing the road.

What he wanted to do was curl up into some kind of cocoon and sleep for another sixteen hours. Maybe he'd get lucky and find a grain cart on the next train out of town. But he'd still have to make his way through another half-hour of walking in the torrents of liquid pneumonia. He stepped back to alcove and sat on the stairs once the man in the jacket was gone. He remembered watching a PBS documentary about monks in Siberia. The monk with his austere beard and stupid wizard's getup had said that there were times when he felt that God had abandoned him, but those were necessary feelings on one's journey toward God. Traveling was Rayne's calling, and today was his first truly bad day. Like the Siberian monk's God, the road had abandoned him and one of its disciples had held a knife to him and tried to cut his throat.

"C'est la vie," Dorn might, have flippantly said to that through cigarette and cheap Scotch breath. He couldn't pronounce French to save his own dick. He'd have said it more like "Say law 'V'." He remembered him there in the kitchen, watching Dorn eat in a white T-shirt and boxers, pouring compulsively from a handle of Old Passport. That was the day he had been suspended for defending himself.

"Look what you did now, kid."

"Yeah, look what I did now, Dorn," he said to himself, an inner dialogue with the great Satan of his life. He snapped himself out of it and thought in his first language, reassessing everything with a fresh idiom.

A police cruiser rolled halfway onto the curb. He made sure the collar of his jacket was zipped all the way and there was nothing red under his fingernails. The front of the cruiser was blocking his escape on the sidewalk, having parked diagonally. The officer swung the door open. She was black with short hair and intense green eyes. She motioned for him to come out of the alcove. He stood up and walked toward her. She had an urgency in her voice, but she wasn't stern or accusing him of anything.

"It's calling of freezing rain. You're gonna get sick."

"Okay," he said, squinting through the downpour.

"Get in the car. I'll take you to the church. They got hot chocolate and bagels."

"That's okay, Ma'am. I'm just leaving town."

"I ain't bustin' you for vagrancy and I ain't tryin' to trick you. A young man like you gets pneumonia and dies on the streets outside of my town, that's bad for business. And this town isn't exactly on the map already except for you travelin' kids."

"Your town?" he said, looking at the badge on her chest.

"Yes, honey. You talkin' to the sheriff. Now, come on. I'll let you sit in the front seat if it makes you feel any better."

"The front seat?"

"Can't nobody tell me nothing. Now, come on. You're gettin' soaked."

He walked around the sidewalk and waited by the passenger door as she leaned over to unlock it for him. He got inside and shook off the cold rain.

She drove them deeper into the town, passing the public library and a rusted out water tower.

"Where is it that you're from?" the sheriff asked him.

"Ohio," he said.

"American? Because you have a little bit of an accent."

"Most people don't hear it," he said. "I've been here so long I can kind of hide it."

"My folks was from Dominica. I know accents. You got something Northern about you. Where are you from?"

"I grew up more or less in Ohio," he said.

"You keepin' it a secret or something?"

"I don't really feel like I'm from there anymore. But I'm not from here either. It feels like a lie."

"That why you on the road?"

"Maybe," he said. "I was born on a little archipelago between Iceland and Norway. It's called The Faroe Islands. My mom had me when she was fifteen. We immigrated to Canada illegally after a while. She worked in a sandwich shop under the table, did all kinds of other stupid shit too, and eventually married this guy in Ohio she met online. A real piece of work. The guy, not her. Then she…"

"Hey, hey. You don't have to tell me your life story. I was just curious. What's your name?"

"I go by Rayne."

"Like Rain?"

"Yeah."

"Have you had anything to eat yet?"

"No," he said.

"You must be hungry."

"I'd rather not go to a church shelter," he said.

"Well, I bet you don't wanna go to the police station either. But those are the only two places I can take you. I ain't dropping you off at the railroad because that's illegal. And this town don't have no bus stop. What you got against Jesus anyway?"

"I don't believe in Jesus."

"Oh, don't give me that bullshit. He believes in you."

6

He sat on the bleachers of the indoor basketball court, a cup of weak coffee in his hand and a banana muffin wrapped in a napkin, trying not to converse with the other down-and-outs accepting food from the church. There was a Mexican family below him and a couple of haggard old drunks on the margins of the echoing space. He ate the last piece of his muffin and drained the coffee before heading to the door. A girl, probably of college age, a volunteer without a doubt, dark hair and uncanny bright eyes, leaned forward over the plastic Coleman pop-up table to give him a pamphlet.

"During the winter months coming up we do a clothing exchange if you need to get something warmer than just that jacket," she said.

"Thanks," he said.

"We're here every Tuesday, but the clothing exchange isn't in the auditorium. It's in the basement down the path. Right next to the playground," she said.

"Appreciate the tip," he said.

He walked out into the sleet with his flimsy jacket. Fuck it. He was already a criminal. He looked around to see who was watching, if there were any homes beyond the brickle trees or if people could spot him from the parking lot, then moved past the playground mired in frozen wet sand like cracked drywall shavings to the door of the church basement. Churches, as he had learned from experience, had subpar security. But today, the door was locked. He scanned the area to make sure no one could see him, then hiked up the wooden steps in the clay to the front doors of the Lutheran chapel. He walked into the vestibule and stared into the darkness of the nave. Pristine. Clean. Maybe some mild dust in the air. The stairwell to the basement was just as dark. It was made of old-world iron, each footfall resounding off the musty concrete walls. He entered the desolate halls of the basement drenched in red light from the exit signs. There was a hospital's sense of quiet in the air as if the commotion of life-and-death urgency which typically roared through the corridors were abated only by the most fragile turn of chance. He slithered into the closet of the youth recreation room and stole an enormous puffy coat. He didn't bother taking off the other jacket and wrapped himself in the immediate warmth. He left the storage area and stepped back into the hall where he noticed the open office door. He could see a cork board on a rolling track. Full color images of four children lifted from family photographs and public school yearbooks. Religious icons peppered the board and above it the marquis read, "Pray for Missing the Parishioners." There were four of them. The memorial had been pushed into the corner of the office. Whoever worked there, understandably, didn't want to file invoices all day under the gaze of dead children. But at its peculiar angle anyone could see it. He took the opportunity to use the restroom stall and wash his face in the sink, then left out the back.

He walked down the road vacant of any traffic, where the ferns and the rhododendrons grew over the highway guards, and imagined that he was in Alaska or the great edge of the Pacific Northwest. He thought about prison, and about the Faroese alphabet. He spoke to himself as he walked. He thought of his father, not Dorn, but the mythical Danish sailor who impregnated his fifteen-year-old mother. He imagined the old man on the road somewhere driving a truck across Germany or drinking in a seaside port on the coast of Norway or Scotland: a real Eurotrash cowboy. What would he say if he met him? Would they look the same, or would he be some blonde cigarette-smoking Viking who had secret kids from Reykjavik to St. Petersburg and no time for anyone other than himself? And how exactly would he let him know he was his son? What proof did he have? He could still speak Faroese, though it was dissipating slowly from his memory every year. And according to his mother, the bastard didn't speak it. He was a blue-collar Dane who could barely get by in English. No, for all the evaporated man would ever know or care to understand, Rayne was just a drifter from Shitkickersville, Ohio. Still, he imagined that meeting.

What looked to him like a hippie bus, some kind of old Volkswagen perhaps, chugged up the winding incline through the mountain fog. The engine popped like a round from a .22 as it drove up beside him. The car wasn't a Volkswagen. It ended up being a Chevy van, something a plumber or a carpet steamer might have driven. The driver rolled down the window and Rayne recognized the girl from last night, the girl at the edge of the underpass taking hits off a straight shooter. She had her soiled-dishwater hair wrapped in a top knot. Beneath her Dickies overalls, which, on her tiny frame, looked like fly-fishing waders, she wore a military green tank top. She blew cigarette smoke like engine steam out the side of her mouth before she spoke.

"You look lost, sojourner."

"You're never lost if you got nowhere to be," he said.

She threw up a hand signal, railcar communication.

Rayne tucked in his index finger with his thumb and covered his right eye with the last three open fingers.

She smiled at him and reached out his hand. They commenced an old West Coast handshake.

They laughed.

"I saw you before I bailed last night," she said.

"I woke up and everybody was gone."

"Nobody spends the night there. It's too open."

"How come nobody woke me up."

"Sleep is a hot commodity. No one's going to take that from another traveler."

"That's true," he said.

"Hop in boy. Come on, what's wrong with you," she said tossing the butt of a cigarette.

He walked around and got into the passenger seat of the car.

"Where are you headed?"

"A friend's place," she said. "Little further up the mountain. It's a cool place to crash."

"Sound's good."

She rolled a quick joint out of some notebook paper like a prison cigarette and sparked up a thumb-sized Bic. The weed had been loose in the cupholder; puffs of dark-broccoli green with orange fibers woven throughout. She offered him a hit and he asked her if there was crack in it.

"Oh, you noticed me last night," she said. "You don't have anything to worry about. It's a pure middle-school cigarette. As soft as the seventies."

She took a hit first.

He gave it a long drag and handed it back. Still holding the smoke in his lungs, he asked her a wheezed question.

"Who's car is this?"

"Guy up the mountain. He let me fuck around with it after I fixed the engine up."

Rayne exhaled.

"*You* fixed it?"

"Yeah, I'm a major tinkerer. 'Specially when I hit a little bit of that crystal," she said. "Crystal. Not crack. I ain't no crackhead."

"You're talking about meth?"

"Don't judge. No judgement here."

"No," he said. "No, judgement. I just wasn't sure you were talking about crank."

"I like to call it amphetamine. You know? Just call stuff what it is. It makes you sound kinda nerdy and square, but… you know fuck it. Weed is cannabis. Acid is LSD baby."

She took another hit off the joint and kept on talking without him.

"So I crash at this guy's lodge up the mountain with a couple of other travelers. He's rich. Not stupid TV rich, but he has a lot of things. And he's down. Like, he knows the rails. I think he traveled when he was younger. He's supposed to be a doctor. Or he used to be a doctor. Honestly, he's kind of like this Hunter S. Thompson type. I think you'll like it quite a bit. You can come and go whenever you want. Stay awhile, or bail tomorrow. It's a great place to get some motherfuckin' rest."

"I don't plan on staying too long," he finally said. "I'm trying to get up to Canada."

"You from there?"

"No," he said. "I'm from Ohio."

"I'm from New Orleans myself."

"What's your name?"

"Jac," she said. "I spell it just 'j' 'a' 'c'."

"I go by Rayne."

"Yeah, I remember from last night."

"Are the same kids at this lodge the ones from the bridge last night?"

"Some of them, yeah."

"Cool," he said, looking out the window.

She took an exit onto a thickly wooded road overrun with icey mud. They passed a series of trailers, some too dilapidated to be occupied; husks of wood and brittle glass windows. Jac was mumbling to herself as she drove. Tree branches swiped at the mirrors as the road grew more narrow. She looked worried.

"You getting too high to drive?"

"I'm just hoping."

"Hoping for what?"

She said nothing. The drive got bumpier. He was starting to feel the cannabis screwing with his center of balance. He couldn't tell how close she was to the edge of the road. The wipers were affecting his view.

"Maybe you should stop and see how we're doing."

She took a brushy curve and hit the brakes. The gate before them was closed, blocking their entry to the remainder of the backwoods road.

"Damn it."

"Do we have to get out to open it?"

"Not if you want him to get to you."

Rayne didn't see anyone at first. His eyes scoured the watery view through the windshield when he heard the brazen churn of a smaller engine. A man on an ATV rolled out through the brush and rhododendron cover. He had on a dark raincoat, thick jeans, and solid boots. He killed the engine and jumped off the ATV, then rolled a piece of tarp over the seat to keep it dry. He stood between them and the gate, looking at them.

"Who's this guy?"

"Pain in the ass. We call him the Cherokee. Thinks he's king of the mountain. According to Cain he owns most the land around here. Inherited it from an old relative. Doesn't like punks. Doesn't do shit but bother people."

He was closing in on the driver's side window, close enough to hear her through the glass. She rolled down the window and he pulled down the hood in spite of the heavy sleet.

He smiled. He was young. Rayne recognized him as what people out West called traditional: a Native American with long hair tucked behind his ears and a beaded necklace tight around his Adam's apple. He spoke with a thick Southern drawl specific to this juncture of Appalachia.

"Howdy," he said.

"Hey ya, hun."

"You folks going up to Cain's?"

"Of course we are," she said.

He looked at Jac then focused his attention on Rayne.

"New to town?"

"If you could call it a town."

"Well, just because it's called Last Junction don't mean it has to be. You'll find more up north. Get'chu to Johnson City, or Knoxville. You'll like it there."

"Till the weather opens up."

"This ain't whether," he said. "Damn sight this ain't weather. You know, Cain's pad must be fun and all but there's gotta be better stuff out there for you travelin' folks."

"We're expected up the mountain, so we're gonna need you to open the gate."

His smile vanished.

"You should turn back. If I were you, I'd turn back."

No one spoke for an even minute.

"But you're not going to," he said. "So, then I'll uh… open up that gate for you. But next time, I can't rightly say I'm gonna be as nice. See, this is private property. This ain't Cain's driveway. I warned ya."

He walked to the gate and unhooked the latch.

"If it was that simple we could have done that?" Rayne said.

"No, you couldn't've."

"Why not? Just drive away, wait for him to leave, then open the thing."

"It isn't as easy as he makes it look. Last kid to try got his hand caught in a trap and lost a finger. This guy's unstable."

"What the fuck?"

She pressed down the gas and pushed the swaying chassis of the van through the narrow gate.

Rayne looked back and watched the young guy get back on his ATV and roll away. He leaned his head back.

"It's been a weird few days," he said.

7

The lodge appeared from the treeline and moss-encrusted boulders like something from a mirage; hearty darkwood steps leading up to a porch that stretched across the entire front of the structure. There were a couple of cars parked askew along the gravel lot, thin sheets of ice beginning to form across their windshields. There was a recycling bin filled with pizza boxes and beer bottle glass beside a bear-proof garbage bin. Frozen windchimes dangled from the far end of the porch. Rayne heard a guitar being strummed when he got out of the van. Another traveler had his feet dangling from a bunk bed just outside the open bay window above the garage.

"Come on," Jac said, pulling him to the back of the property.

There was a tall man in a blue flannel shirt and gloves standing in the woods, setting empty liquor bottles on a series of worn stumps.

"Hey, Jac," he said.

"Hey, this is Rayne. He's going to Canada. Needs a place to stay tonight."

"Sure, the upstairs has got some vacancy," he said, then tossed a loaded clip at Rayne. "Think fast."

Rayne caught it with one hand.

"What is this a 9mm."

"Very good."

Cain, assuming that this man was Cain, had wild gray hair and reminded him of something more like Christopher Lloyd than Hunter S. Thompson if it weren't for the Yosemite Sam mustache.

"You wanna do some shootin'?"

"Okay, sure" he said.

"You ever fired a gun before?"

"No."

"You ever killed a man where he stood?"

Rayne raised an eyebrow, "What do you know?"

Cain looked at him as he took out the gun from his belt loop. "I know everything, son," he said, then burst into laughter. "I'm just joshin' ya. I'm kinda drunk already off a few beers and some sangria. Hand me that clip there, son."

Rayne tossed it back against his better judgement. There was a drunk old man now standing in the falling ice with a loaded handgun.

He gave the gun to Rayne and switched the safety back with his long index finger. "Hit the bottles."

Rayne looked around and noticed Jac had disappeared into the warmth of the lodge. He squeezed the trigger and felt the thunderous round crack in his numbed hand as the muzzle flash and smoke trail poured from the barrel and, in the split-second retraction to eject the false-tooth colored shell casing, the slide as well. The bullet hit the stump just beneath the liquor bottle. Chips of wood sprayed upward. The bottle was unmoved.

"Not quite," Cain said. "Raise it a bit."

He fired again. The bottle shattered.

"Good shot. I think you earned yourself a couple of beers."

"Thanks," he said, handing the gun back to the old man.

He walked inside through the sunroom, letting the screen door slap the frame behind him as he stepped into the warm kitchen. There was a golden Buddha on the granite countertop island next to a bowl of over-ripe fruit. He listened to the gunshots from Cain's 9mm as they hacked away at the frozen tufts of elephant grass beyond the yard. He had found a place to stay, a warm hideaway of like-minded people, a place that would have meant so much more to him at the beginning of his travels. Still, here with all these wayward people, caricatures of themselves, he was alone. The blood of a murderer ran through his veins. He thought of the Buddha and how many other seekers had returned from their sojourn with nothing, not even themselves. How many young princes had been eaten by tigers on the path to enlightenment? Could the Buddha have killed someone if he woke up beneath the Bodi tree and they had a dagger to his throat? That's what he would have asked him. And what *of* Jesus Christ? What would he have done if instead of himself, they had chosen to crucify his mother? It was the truth of the path, the treachery of the journey which he had had to confront head on. He knew, even within his guilt and confusion, that he had done the right thing. While no kindly sweater-vested therapist could absolve him of the trespass, no other human being would ever know the depth of innocence either.

To his right, he noticed the open closet full of hiker's backpacks stamped with punk rock patches. Jac stood behind him.

"You can put your shit away if you want."

"Rather not," he said.

"Grab a beer and come chill in the living room."

"If it's all the same, I need to crash."

"Hell, yeah. Upstairs second door to the left."

"Thanks."

He moved through the hallway crowded with ugly knick-nacks and rock'n'roll memorabilia and headed upstairs. Elaborate railcar tags and graffiti covered the walls of the narrow corridor. Cain had allowed the traveler to turn his home into a squat. What was in it for him? Drugs? Sex? A family? He entered the room lined with bunk beds. The man had created his own *jugendherberge*. What was the Faroese word? He didn't know. The kid hanging out the window was still raking his fingers across the nylon strings. Rayne crawled into a free bed and passed out.

8

He woke up curled in the old blanket, arms numb and wrapped around his backpack. The bay window was still open. No sign of the guitar player. The rain and sleet fell sideways in the wind like static electrical signals freed into the ether, shaking the tree limbs loose. Someone else sat upright in the bunk next to his, a young boy with almost no punk iconography on him. He smoked a cigarette and watched the rain.

"And who the fuck are you?" the kid said without looking at him.

"Nobody," Rayne said.

"When did you get in?"

"I hitched a ride with Jac earlier."

"Figures," the kid said. "You ever stared at something so long you don't recognize it anymore."

"No."

"Shows you how fragile your own certainty is. Your eyes aren't telling you the truth. Your eyes are like a blind man's fingers trying to read braille on a jagged rock."

He took a long drag on the cigarette. The ember glowed a weak orange before he exhaled.

"You ever see a dead man weep?"

"I don't really know what that means."

"Have you ever been to a haunted house?"

"Like where people jump out at you?"

"No, like a real place where people were killed."

The kid must have been high.

"How would I know?"

He ignored Rayne's question.

"If you look into these forests long enough, you can see the ghosts of all the people who were forced out."

Rayne stood up, still wrapped in the blanket, and closed the giant window. Freezing water had poured inside and soaked the edge of the closest bunk. "That's enough ghosts for one night."

He turned back and the kid was gone. The bunk he had been sitting in had melting ice and mud streaked across the sheets. Wet shoe prints trailed into the hallway. He followed them and when the hall was too dark to see, followed the scent of the smoke. He went down the stairs and into the kitchen. Cain's 9mm sat, fully loaded, beside the pretentious golden Buddha. He didn't want to eat but his stomach churned with hunger. He opened the fridge and drank a Coca-Cola, then ate four hot dogs from the sealed pack in the crisper.

"Let me heat those up for you, son."

Cain was standing behind him sipping a hot cup of coffee, smoking a cigarette. It was almost eight o'clock in the evening. He wore an old pajama robe with slippers, exposing his thin legs.

"I've got mustard and relish. You gotta have a ballpark frank the right way, you dig?"

"I don't want to trouble you."

"No problemo, I'm not doing anything. Just got up from my nap."

"Really, it's okay."

The old man pointed at him with his index and middle finger, holding the cigarette, and punctuated each word with a short
interval. "Sit… your… ass… down."

Rayne took a seat at the island.

"Jesus," Cain said as he took the hot dogs from the fridge
and began placing them in the George Foreman grille. "You kids.
Sometimes you forget how to accept help, you know. It's rough
out there. Not in here."

"I suppose you're right," Rayne said, a prisoner on the bar
stool.

"Yeah, people are crazy all over. So what's your story. Where
are you from?"

"Ohio."

"Anywhere close to Cleveland?"

"No south Ohio. The boonies. West Virginia border."

"You born there?"

"No."

"Where were you born?"

When Cain turned his back to search through the cupboard,
Rayne swiveled the barrel of the pistol away from himself on the
counter.

"The Faroe Islands."

"God damn, that's one I haven't heard yet," he said, pulling
hotdog buns from the top shelf. "I've got whole wheat and gluten
free. No, white bread bromated shit though. That okay?"

"Whole wheat sounds fine."

"But does it sound good? You're my guest, man. Go nuts.
You want another Coke? A beer? Jack and Coke? I got Jack Dan-
iels in the liquor cabinet."

He grabbed another Coke from the fridge.

Cain fished the condiments from the fridge door.

"You like relish?"

"Yeah."

"You ever had Sabrett's. That red onion relish they put on hotdogs."

"No."

"No? You're from the North."

"Can't say I ever heard of it."

"It's great. It's old school ballpark stuff. I miss it. I'm originally from New York myself. Went to med school in Pennsylvania. I practiced in Pennsylvania for a long time. Then I retired here. Practiced a little. Not much, though. But that's boring shit. We don't have to talk about those days."

"What kind of doctor were you?"

"Pediatrics," he said.

Rayne said nothing else and sat in silence while the old man placed ketchup, mustard and relish on the hotdogs. He served them on a cobalt blue china plate.

"You smoke?"

Rayne nodded.

The old man gave him a filtered Camel and a lighter.

"For when you're finished. Eat up."

He lit himself another and stepped out of the room.

Jac passed through the kitchen.

"You're gettin' the star treatment, Bud."

Her eyes were dilated as if she were high on triple Cs. He didn't know too much about whatever she might have taken, but she appeared too sluggish to have done any crank. She stumbled out of the kitchen. Rayne finished his food and lit the cigarette. He washed the single dish in the sink, letting the cigarette dangle from his lip, staring out into the semi-darkness of the backyard.

He continued to smoke as he crept through the enormous living room. Cain was sorting through his vinyl record collection. Jac walked passed him to stoke the logs in the fireplace, bending forward to grab the poker. That's when Cain reached over, still looking through his records, and gave her ass cheek an open-handed swat. She smiled back at him as though it were an innocent gesture. Four other travelers were looking right at them and didn't react. She stoked the fire and closed the metal grating, then fell backward into the couch beside two other guys. Rayne scanned the room. He still didn't see the kid from upstairs. He found an ashtray and stubbed out his cigarette. Night was falling fast beyond the windows and he'd be trapped in this house for several more hours.

He belched from the two Cokes. It had been so long since he had had anything carbonated to drink. Even the many beers along the way, which had always been salvaged and hustled like the commodity they were, came to his lips each time nearly flat. He wandered through the halls of the house, used the bathroom, and holed up in the small library. Not too many medical books on the shelves, mostly novels and rock'n'roll biographies. Cain was a Dead Head as it turned out. Pictures of Bob Weir and Jerry Garcia peppered the margins of the book spines. There was a book already open on the mantle: Hiking the trails of North Carolina. He read for a few minutes, looking at the Appalachian Trail and everything else connected by it. He listened to the others laugh in the living room and devised a plan to sleep again as best he could anyway, then leave at dawn.

He bummed another cigarette off of Jac this time and went upstairs, smoking the cheap brand of harsh, tasteless tobacco. He was in a reading mood still and lingered in the hallway, reading the railcar tags. It was hard to read them in the dark. He went for the light switch, but the bulb must have been burned out. He squinted to read at large tag carved into the doorframe of the bunk room:

It meant "Get out while you still can, danger here."

"Shit," he said aloud.

He dropped the cigarette to the bare floor and stomped it out, then peered into the bunk room. The bay window, as he remembered, hadn't been too high from the ground.

He pulled his backpack around and stood on the bunk closest to the glass, then opened the window to a cold burst of sleet, as if it were the hatch to some nautical vessel, and used his pack as a cushion for his fall.

His knees went limp on the first false start.

He had jumped from a moving train before, he could do this.

The wind smacked his face as the sill dropped beneath his feet. The impact was minimal.

He landed atop the hood of the van and slid off into the icy gravel. He put on his cap and wrapped the straps of the pack around his stolen coat. The lights of the house disappeared behind the rocks. The scent of firewood smoke in the atmosphere was strong. He wondered how long it might take him to freeze to death, his eyes adjusting to the darkness.

He was accompanied only by his footfalls on the asphalt and the rain as he returned to the invisible margins of the world, his home.

9

He could make it. He thought he could. Fleeting notions of grandiosity were enough to lie to himself to get to the next challenge. Maybe those internal lies would sustain him? But only in the ferocity of a paranoid mind do the proverbial scales tip both ways simultaneously in that unholy headspace where pros become cons and advantages read as synonymous with brutal handicap. What kind of story would it be? How he survived the cold of the night, or how they (whoever they were) would find him?

He considered Golem's body freezing in the sewage pipe.

"Fuck!"

The body would never decompose in a freeze .

But Rayne, the devil within said, nature isn't keeping the evidence. It's doing you a favor. He freezes in the stream and doesn't surface till spring. Who then could know the time of death? People won't have seen you here for months by then, and you'll be gone

Maybe, he thought. But didn't it feel so goddamned sheepish to worry about a self-defense murder when it was the right thing to do? The notion of confession tugged at him: just go back to the Sheriff and admit to what he had done. No. She'd never believe him. He rode the rails. He was scum. He had to walk a different path now.

He walked down a steep portion of the road and saw the hair-pin turn at the very bottom lit up by hazard lights. The orange crimson glow reflected off the municipal yellow of the danger sign and sharp-curve-left arrows. The trees seemed to wrap around each end of the safety guards, meeting at the top like an alcove or a man-made arch. The darkness of his world was now pierced by color, a strange beacon toward which he moved. The rain pelted the windshield and hood of the small black Cadil-lac. He inspected the scene from a distance at first. The driver's side door had been left open, stopped halfway against the steel safety guard half shrouded in solid black foliage. The sedan was parked diagonally, allowing space for passing traffic. The asphalt, what part he could see in the flickering light, was streaked with tire tread. He chose to move closer, attempting to see if the front crashed in. He could feel his cheeks flush as his heart raced. An old man in a sweater appeared to be wandering around the road at the front of the vehicle. The front left headlight was smashed and the hood of the car slightly wrinkled. A low impact colli-sion. The old man had probably lost control of the car. This was his chance to be a good samaritan. He raised his hands up and approached him.

"Sir? Are you already?" his tongue slipped.

"Alright? Are you alright? What happened?"

The old man looked at him like he had seen him before.

"Were you the guy?"

"Who?"

"I saw a guy. I thought I hit him. I thought I…" He stared off into the trees and thought he saw something in the dark. "The guy. The guy. I saw him driving. When I was driving, I mean."

"I just got here. I was coming down the road." He ges-tured toward the road behind him and inspected the front of the Cadillac. "You've got nothing to worry about. You didn't hit anybody. You hit the steel girder thing there, but nobody is hurt."

"Was it you?"

"No," Rayne said. "I'm fine it's not me. Are you okay?"

"I… I… I've gotta get home," the old man said moving around the car. "My daughter. She's sick. She's in the hospital."

He thought about the old man driving out here in the middle of the night to get to his daughter. He was confused and afraid, barely able to negotiate the mountain roads at his age. Poor bastard.

"I get it, man. I really do, but you might have hurt yourself when you hit the side there."

"I'm only on shore leave for another twelve hours. If I don't get there I won't see her again."

Rayne said nothing in disbelief.

The old man grabbed Rayne's shoulders.

"She's just a few months old. I didn't get to see her born. I don't know what she looks like."

Rayne forced the old man's hands off him and took the old man by the elbow.

"Come with me. We're gonna get you some help, okay?"

He took him to the car and tried to get him to take a seat out of the rain.

"She's just a few months old."

"I know. I know," Rayned said.

He wouldn't sit and continued to wander around the road.

"I know I saw a guy. He was here. He had no skin. His eyes must always be open."

"I need you to calm down, sir. Do you have a phone?"

"A phone?"

"Yeah, like a cellphone?"

"Ah jeez. Ah darn. Look, fella if you had shown up any later our asses would be smoke by now. You're a good man, you know that?"

"Thank you. So do you have a phone?"

"What vessel you serve on?"

"Fuck it."

He walked over to the car and started looking through the glove compartment and the floor for a cellphone. An old black-berry. A Jitterbug. Anything. Rayne suddenly felt himself being pulled back by his backpack with an unusual amount of force. The rain-soaked, brittle fist of the man came down on him, knocking him to the ground only because he had lost his center of balance. He landed comfortably on his pack and rolled to the side like a turtle. Once he was back on his feet, the dementia stricken man ran back toward him. Trying to grasp at the collar of his coat.

"Get the fuck out of my car, you punk."

Rayne did what he could to push the man away without hurt-ing him. The elderly hands gripped his neck. He could feel the ex-sailor's thumbs pressing his Adam's apple, pushing into the soft scar from earlier.

Headlights approached from up the incline. Hopefully they wouldn't be too shocked or afraid to stop and help him placate the old man.

He forced his hands off of him and pushed him against the soaked hood of the car.

The high beams set everything in their path ablaze as the vehicle barreled down the hill.

"You're trying to kill me!" the old man said.

"I'm trying to help you, now sit the fuck down."

He left the man sitting on the hood and stepped before the lights, waving his hand.

The old man stood up and ran toward him in a frenzy, knocking into him like a linebacker.

The lights hurtled toward the old man.

Rayne rolled away, struggling to move quickly enough across the asphalt, kicking the old man away with his feet.

The large vehicle slowed and eventually braked.

Rayne got to his feet and began yelling for help.

No one emerged from the vehicle. Rightly so, he thought. Who the hell wanted to deal with this mess at night? If he just had two seconds to calmly explain, they'd know it wasn't as bad as it looked. He walked over to the old man and helped him up. He didn't put up a fight. Rayne took him back to the Cadillac and sat him down in the passenger's seat with the door open, at least halfway out of the rain. He looked back at the blinding lights and called out to the driver.

"You can stay in your car, that's fine. But this man has dementia. I need you to call 911 if you have a cellphone."

A cold silence. The engine rumbled.

"Can you hear me? Just call 911 for us and you can be on your way. Please?" He tried to speak as loud as he could. "If you understand, turn down your lights."

He waited a few moments.

The high beams shut off.

He could see the large vehicle's outline now in the dark: a black SUV. He thought of the two porcelain eyes staring back at him through the windshield that previous night. This couldn't have been the one. Black SUVs were common.

"Thank you," he yelled out.

A few seconds passed. The old man appeared to have been temporarily placated. Rayne was about to get inside the Cadillac for shelter when the driver's side windshield of the SUV finally rolled down.

He walked toward the vehicle, but didn't approach the open window. He didn't want to scare the driver.

"Hey, thanks for stopping. I just found this guy on the side of the road," he said, trying to get a glimpse of the driver.

In the strong light of the iPhone mounted near the steering wheel with the navigation app still running, he could see the kind face of a young woman. She had blonde hair and short glasses.

"I called 911. It might take awhile," she said in a panicked voice. "I'm going to pull onto the shoulder here as best I can but I'm locking the doors. You should get inside your car and do the same."

"Okay. You're right."

"Keep him in the car. I almost ran over you both."

"I just wanted to say thank you," Rayne said.

"You didn't give me much of a choice."

Her remark ended abruptly as both of them reacted to a gaseous noise beneath their feet as if a valve in the engine had burst. The right side of the SUV sloped toward Rayne. He stared down at the flattening tire and noticed what at first looked like a stick lodged firmly in its slick, black rubber, then, once it was too late, he saw the fletching and nock of a common department-store arrow. A second immediately struck the woman in her neck, pinning her against the vinyl headrest at an oblique angle. Her liquified gasp pulled up a thin streak of blood that coursed down her chin. Rayne took cover behind the old man's Cadillac. Another arrow cracked the windshield of its open door. The old man raced from the car back into the open.

"He's here! He's here!"

An arrow lodged into his kneecap.

Rayne watched as his leg twisted, ligaments tearing, before he fell flat on the ground.

Three more arrows pierced the man's back as he dragged himself away, screaming in agony.

Rayne's mind raced. It was the Cherokee wasn't it?

The figure approached the SUV and reached inside the window to shut off the engine and take the keys. His back looked heavy with the quiver of arrows and the massive mechanical crossbow slung over his shoulder with two leather straps. The shooter's body was covered in hunting camouflage. He saw his green fingerless gloves as he pulled open the car door and dragged the woman from her seat. He heard the arrow's muffled snap somewhere close to her neck. She sat on the asphalt, her back against the side of her vehicle. The camouflaged figure took his time.

It wasn't the Cherokee.

When he finally caught a good look at the shooter's face, he wasn't sure what he saw. A lipless mouth with teeth exposed. No nose to speak of. Wet tufts of hair across the ears. Beady eyes keen on the woman as the rain washed away her throat's profuse bleeding. The hunter plucked a near-sword length Bowie knife from the leather sheath affixed to his belt and swiped the blade into the side of her skull. It penetrated her face by several inches reaching her eye. He set his boot on her shoulder for leverage and jerked the handle of the knife upward as routinely as one might remove a knife from a branch, bringing up a flurry of chopped hair and skin.

He watched as the hideous face turned to the old man. To avoid him, Rayne crawled into the mud beneath the warped safety railing. The hunter stepped over to the old man. His footfalls appeared to part the rain around the rubber of his boots. The old man raised up an arm to drag himself further. The hunter knelt down on one knee and drove the knife through his shoulder. The screams were muffled. He was losing his stamina. The hunter gripped the handle and began to saw through the skin and layers of clothing. Rayne struggled to get a hold of his footing. A rock dislodged beneath him. His hands lost their grip on the rhododendron branch and he slid down into the freezing mud of the gulch. He landed on his backpack looking back up at the road. In the end, it was a quick escape. Better to run now while whatever it was he had seen was still preoccupied with mutilating the old man. He rolled back onto his feet and ran toward the brush. What had looked to be a plateau was a steep drop and he fell rapidly, snapping every tenuous branch in his way as if several whips had struck him in succession bloodying his face and ears. He snapped a young poplar on impact, almost skewering his abdomen. Once he had landed, he lifted himself to his feet and walked slowly through the underbrush, making sure he hadn't broken anything.

He reached out for one of the tree silhouettes, balancing himself. Out here, in the depths of the woods, the earth stood blacker than the depthless chasm of the sky and at night the canopy seemed outlined by the last handful of photon particles to ricochet off the surface of the human eye. The dim, shuddering grayness overhead did nothing to guide him. He tore his feet free of the suction made by the still unfrozen mud. Every step a struggle, he moved deeper into the wilderness.

10

The freezing rain had stopped. A small pattern of heat must have moved into the region now that he saw the firmament open up with long slashes of wiry, ecstatic light. Thunder broke just overhead like the awakening of a giant. He had always paid attention to the weather. For some, weather was the background to an otherwise consistent lifestyle. But when you lived on the road, and by proxy, the street: a much less seductive way to describe homelessness, self-imposed or otherwise, the elements had to become your home. It must have been something like being a farmer, but for him the earth didn't yield its fruits, it was just his transportation. He rode the grass and the dirt, the asphalt and the gravel. Traveling on the earth meant the earth moved with you. But it wasn't until his recent days that he realized the earth could also move against you.

Rayne stood on a level segment of rock about seven, possibly eight feet, from a raging creek and caught a glimpse of the terrain in the flashes of lightning. Wind bellowed through the valley, carrying moisture that pelted his cuts and bruises. There was a tin roof shed on the opposite side, close to the treeline. He would have to ford the water. For his purposes the babbling creek was now an immense river. He followed the bank to see if there were any rocks he could run across, maybe an easy bend where the water narrowed and he could jump.

There appeared to be a line of smoothed-over rock where the water, at least in the sudden flash of lightning, appeared to be shallow enough to run across. If he slipped, which was more than likely, he'd get even wetter than he was now the way the water would soak into his socks and underwear, then, shelter or not, he'd get cold and probably end up with pneumonia. Was it worth it just to find shelter; some hillbilly's meth shack where he'd probably get bitten by a rabid coyote lost in the storm? His legs made the decision before his mind was completely made up. He raced across the line of rock, teetered precariously near the end, and dove headlong on to the opposite bank. He stepped through the waist-high brush and approached the shack. He wanted to make a fire and wondered if the matches in his pack had gotten wet.

He stood before the door of the shed. There was a window beside it looking out to the miniature porch. The glass had been shattered years ago. Wild sweet potato vines and constricting weeds had tangled their way up the frame. He grabbed the wooden handle and opened the door. The floor had become so filthy it may as well have been dirt. He had no light but the sudden flash of lightning was enough for him to see the fireplace in the corner: a brief glimpse of dark red brick streaked with black. There were scraps of dry wood everywhere. He broke off pieces of vine and table until he had assembled a small bundle of kindling. He scooped up a handful of sawdust from the work table and did his best to set it in the middle of the stack since he had no paper. He took a deep breath and fished through his pack to find the matches. The hotel matches from Nebraska were soaked, but his box from Walmart seemed intact. He struck one and set it in his bundle. The sawdust went up like gunpowder, too fast for the wood to catch the flame. He took another scoop of sawdust and ripped the paper backing off his hotel matchbook. He dried it off and lit another match, waiting for the paper to catch. Once he had a tall flame he set it in the kindling bundle, then sprinkled the sawdust over it. He had a reasonable fire going when he added the two halves of a broken sawhorse.

He stared into the flames and marveled at his ingenuity. Fire was tricky for travelers. He'd heard a lot about people dying in their sleep from smoke inhalation and kids burning down their squats. The key was to make sure you knew where the smoke was headed and to keep the flames contained in something far away from trash or chemicals, which was never easy.

He dried himself off in the heat.

Water dripped inside from a hole in the roof somewhere closer to the center of the shack. Before he let his guard down, he set another small pile of wood on the makeshift fire. He got his sleeping bag once his clothes were reasonably dry and tried to sleep. It was an old trick he had learned in Oregon. Depending on how soaked through your clothes were, it was sometimes best to dry them while still wearing them, otherwise the clothing became bunched and itchy. It could be like wearing sandpaper.

The warming fire lit up the back of the shack. In the dim, flickering light, he saw four piles of stone, or what vaguely looked something akin to four stone totems. Startled, he stood up and let his eyes adjust. They weren't totems or even made of stone. He was staring at four trash bags piled in the corner. He leaned his head back and took a deep breath.

11

Rayne had two grandparents whom he had never met. His mother, whose stories were prevarications at best when she wasn't telling outright lies about his past, used to tell him that her parents were caviar and herring industry moguls as well as hellfire Calvinists. When she got pregnant and dropped out of school, they shunned her from the family and cut her out of the estate. Poor little rich girl, he thought. It was a nice dream at least. Somewhere overseas in that mythical landscape between the seaside rocks and cow pastures, there was a pair of sad old Faroese people who couldn't fathom what their imaginary grandson could have become at the hands of their stupid and dangerously impulsive daughter. They didn't even know she was dead. She had been sick for weeks around the time he had just started high school, pneumonia or the flu. He had never really gotten a straight answer, probably because she didn't know herself. In a world of pinpoint diagnosis, for those who were too stubborn or destitute to see a doctor an illness could be as elusive as magic. And of course, she had gone against Rayne's suggestion to stop drinking when she was ill, slowly dehydrating herself and prolonging the symptoms. Another few days went by and Dorn was still working her like an old mule. She was cleaning clothes and cooking when she wasn't coughing or sitting up in bed with a bottle of Dayquil and glass of Ezra Brooks and soda. She was losing weight, which she was thrilled at, finally shedding the extra pounds she had put on since coming to the United States. But it was all adding up. Dorn seldom let his mom off the hook for anything. That included her nightly degradation. Punk rock and thrash metal were the typical remedy. Rayne could blast the music to drown out the pounding on the wall and squeaking of the bed frame. She screamed a lot. It was the screaming that pierced the music. Her protests out of anger would startle him out of his trance and he would simply turn the music up. The music also drowned out her crying, which he never wanted to listen to. There was always blood in the sheets and fresh tubes of hemorrhoid cream by the toilet. In the end, she had gotten the last laugh on Dorn. Rayne had to think of it that way. He had no other choice. It was the one memory he distanced himself from: seeing her lying there in the bed naked, the strange way the blood pooled to the back of her body causing her lips to turn blue as she stared at the ceiling fan, the fact that he hadn't heard any screaming through the wall for some time, just Dorn's heavy, masochistic grunts. That's how he knew. For a minimum of three entire minutes, an eternity for this sort of thing, before he fell off the bed yelling for his life, Dorn had been so self absorbed that he failed to notice he was screwing a corpse.

The ordeal of the night had just begun. He talked to EMTs, police officers, grief counselors, and other mysterious officials whose jobs and titles he couldn't quite place. He even heard a few of them snicker behind closed doors. She was gone. After that he stopped trying in school, started taking day trips to neighboring towns with others in the punk crowd, smoking a little dope once in a while. He had been preparing himself for the road ahead.

The trailer was never clean after that day. He washed what he wanted clean when he needed it and told Dorn to fuck himself if he asked him to put a load of his on. The washing machine broke three days before Rayne hit the road. He didn't steal any money from Dorn. That would've ensured Dorn coming after him. Dorn. God damn it, Dorn. Dorn, the reluctant necrophile.

12

He could hear breathing.

The fire had died down, providing its most warmth yet, having turned into a glowing ball of deep red coals. He had, for once, achieved some level of comfort and managed to sleep for what seemed like a significant portion of the night. The birds outside weren't chirping and the dew hadn't yet settled, but the storm was gone. An uneasy quiet fell over the holler. The dripping from the roof was intermittent. And he heard breathing. Soft, effortless breaths accompanied by the noise of plastic.

He turned over on his other side, head still firmly planted on the pack as if it were a pillow, and looked over at the plastic bags. Of the four, only one remained and it was moving, a portion of the plastic sucked inward conforming to the shape of the mouth with each breath. He stood up and packed his things.

The breathing stopped.

He took a length of dead Carolina bamboo and poked at the bag. The top came undone and all he saw inside were old newspapers and paint cans.

He pissed on the fire and strapped on his backpack, taking the bamboo as a walking stick as he stepped through the door.

For whatever reason, he had Metallica's *Fade to Black* stuck in his head. He had been imagining his old record collection, the milk crate left under the Ohioan underpass like the Ark of the Covenant.

He didn't know where he was in relation to the road anymore, and what good had the road done him anyway? He kept walking past the shack, traversing the tallgrass.

He thought back to the derelict chapel, the one in Omaha where he lost his virginity. The girl from Montana had talked to him all night long while they drank cheap Vodka and ate canned sausage. She was adamant she had communicated with ghosts.

"Like telepathically?" he had said.

"As plain as you and me are talking now. It's a once in a lifetime thing. A ghost is usually only seen in passing. If you're open enough, and brave enough to exchange two words with one, it's like making contact with an alien race."

"And you've had a conversation with a ghost?"

"No," she had said. "I didn't say that. I've just communicated with one. I was trespassing on the Crow Reservation. I didn't know it at the time. You cross enough fences and barriers, you don't know where the fuck you are. But nobody wants to see a drifter white girl on their land. I was walking along the road and I could see a farmhouse in the distance. I figured I'd sneak into the barn and spend the night. I was about halfway there when I saw this little boy, this little Crow boy with gray pants and a white shirt and old leather suspenders. His hair was cut real short, and he ran across the road with a switch in his hand, just playing in the field, no shoes. I asked him if it was his farm up the road. And… he looked at me with this curious look… like he was surprised I was there, then he waved to me. When I waved back, the instant I waved back, the headlights of a cop car came down the road and in the headlights the kid dematerialized. I mean, I saw his body turn see-through and disappear like he was a smudge on a window getting wiped away."

"What happened then?"

"I didn't dare tell the cop I saw it. He'd have thought I was high or something. The tribal police picked me up and drove me to the bus stop. They packed my ass up out of there. Gave me a break though and didn't fine me for vagrancy."

"He couldn't have anyway. Non-tribal members can't be convicted of crimes on a reservation."

"This cop could've though. I bet he could've. 'Cause I saw on his uniform the patch said U.S. Department of Interior or something."

He never saw that girl again. He wondered if she had gotten pregnant. It was possible. Then she'd run off to a foreign country with her American son and marry some dumb-ass and the cycle continued. Perhaps then his biological father was adrift like him, looking for spiritual clarity.

He wandered back into the forest, stepping over mossy rocks and gnarled roots. He smelled smoke in the distance, a campfire. He followed the scent. It must have been made fresh; no fire would survive the storms that just fell over the region. A home, he thought. That was the only explanation. Someone had a fire going in their home. He pushed past wet bushes and kept his shoes out of the thawing mud, using the bamboo stick to check its depth. He approached a smaller clearing, almost a holler, nestled in the arches of two foothill-sized inclines where the pines were smaller. There was more space for him to stand now, and the ground leveled beneath the carpet of silt and ice and interwoven pine needles. The smoke was strongest here. At first glance, as he came down the bramble-covered slope, he thought he saw the smoke itself lingering in the air. He walked through the valley sniffing audibly. He looked toward the foothill before him and squinted at the horizon, trying to spot a chimney plume.

Nothing.

He moved along, heading upward. He caught his breath once, halfway up the hill. It was at the top of the peak, where he caught a good look at the rolling hills and distant mountains surrounding him, that he found an orange trail blaze carved into a series of thin poplars. He followed the neon orange along the ridge to a metal spike hammered into the wrinkled bark of a towering oak. From the spike hung a reflective orange octagon of plastic, catching the first few lights of morning. Beyond that he noticed an open air cabin at the base of the ridge. The sign above read "Camp Jackson."

Graffiti covered the plywood boards which lined the base of the gazebo-like structure as if they had once been the walls long since removed and strewn across the ground to rot. Beneath his feet were the remnants of the gravel path now punctuated by bland stretches of empty clay earth and overgrown weeds. Cobwebs and active spider homes with translucent flecks of morning dew caught in their fractal geometry proliferated along the roof. Stapled to the beam closest to the conifer-branch-specked eave was a scout itinerary. He read through the activities: lunch, flint workshop, campsite cleanup, wilderness excursion, free recreation. It was a goddamned kid's camp.

He kept on, following what was left of the gravel path until he began to see other squat buildings amid the overgrown broomsedge and rhododendrons. Some of them still had wooden signs hanging from rusted chains above the doors. Each little cabin had a different tribal name carved into it: Cherokee, Dakota, Mohawk, Blackfoot. Nothing too difficult for a child to pronounce. Still consciously following the scent of the smoke, he stopped at the steps of the largest cabin yet. The shingles were sliding off the roof, making way for bird's nests. He checked the cobblestone chimney for signs of smoke but saw nothing. There were glass windows on this cabin through which he could still see nothing. There was a shitty totem pole at the fork in the trail. It looked to have been carved with an electric saw blade at some roadside attraction. The faces almost looked Japanese in their kabuki-style grins; nothing like the eagle designs of the Pacific Northwest. He took a seat on a nearby log and watched the sunrise.

It was obvious the camp had been abandoned for some time. Anyone squatting around here, stoking a fire was not a friend. Not this far from the tracks.

There were two trail blaze marks on the wings of the knock-off totem pole, one for each path at the fork. He went to the right, away from his perceived origin of the smoke, and continued to follow the orange blaze. He spotted a campsite overcome with sassafras leaves and poison sumac. There were sitting logs and a metal fire pit with retractable grating, but no evidence of a recent fire. He stood away from the poison leaves atop of the log and pushed back the grating with the bamboo stick, then poked and stirred through the gray carbon ash.

The noise of a distant bird startled him.

Down the path, where the land dropped into a lower elevation, he could see an immense formation of boulders and a narrow passage between them. As he got closer, he saw a smattering of orange paint on the side of the rock. He ducked under and passed through. What at first looked like a candy bar wrapper on the cold stone steps leading to the end of the passage turned out to be half of an Eagle Scout patch. The patch was destroyed, its fibers melted away into a tough plastic crust. He inspected it for a few seconds then set it back onto the stone. He scaled the stone steps and emerged from the boulders. The word "Tsali" had been carved into the stone with some kind of high powered machine, or perhaps even a chisel. Across from the boulder were two massive elms. Each had one word etched in block letters: "FORGIVE and "U.S." He immediately noticed the word 'us' had what appeared to be two periods as though it were initials, but it had been so long since the words had been fresh. The trees had healed over the slashes, warping the words. He looked beyond the trees and, in the gulch shaded by stray leaves of an Empress of China, he saw twelve shallow graves all marked with stick crosses. At least four had been dug up by animals and were now empty. What at first looked like a wasp nest was actually the top half of a human skull sunken halfway in the dirt and dead leaves. He stepped into the gulch and picked up the skull. It was small, soft ball sized. He returned it to the ground and continued to follow the trail. Just above the treeline, he saw a circling of black vultures, and thought to himself that perhaps where there was death there might be roadkill and he could return to the highway. He was getting tired again and starting to feel the hunger return. Perhaps the road was too dangerous. It hadn't served him well so far, but, as he considered his options, he knew he couldn't stay in the woods without losing his ability to think rationally. His mind, always piecing together the multiplying branches of all possible narratives, had already been challenged to the point of psychotic fatigue. There was a terrifying possibility surfacing. The disappearing bags in the shack. He could have been hallucinating those. But not what happened on the road. That was no hallucination. Or was it? The cabins. The skull. Had he been holding a rock thinking it was the remains of a slaughtered child? The messages. Had he seen what he wanted to see?

Was he schizophrenic?

It was a valid and rational question.

And if so, was he a danger to people around him? Why not? He had already killed a man, he thought.

He followed the vultures as they hovered above like a smoke signal. There was no roadkill, no interstate highway, not even a back road. But he finally traced the origin of the smoke. He approached the outskirts of a large, makeshift camp, having first seen a length of rope tied around two maple trunks on which a dry pair of well-worn jeans and a few long-john shirts hung. A fire raged under a steel tripod where an enameled pot of coffee brewed and a bubbling tin of stew had been balanced on the edge of the circular grating. The flatbed of a truck with a connected roof opened up into a small living area with blankets, a short stack of books, and other belongings. Just beyond the stationary truck, he saw a blue plastic rain barrel and a patio chair facing the distance. He stayed a few feet back, scanning the camp for the owner when he saw the reason for the vultures overhead: a beaver carcass hung by its feet from a rope the same as the clothesline, gutted and bled like a deer. Still no sign of the forest hermit.

He watched the camp, waiting for someone to appear, anyone, as he crouched in the leaves. Back to the war in his head, the secret Vietnam all his own. There was a faint ringing of static syncopating with the gaseous hardwood smolder of the fire and, as he drew closer, with the caution of a soldier in a war zone, of course, he noticed that the static came from the truck radio. A few lengths of copper wiring had been strung up inside the radio and looped within a pair of jumper cables connected to a battery like some kind of grade school science experiment. The car battery sat in the passenger's seat of the truck. Acidic discharge coursed down the sides of the battery like dried milk, burning an outline into the fabric. The static went in and out, playing truncated pieces of a Holy Roller broadcast: "Adults! Where are the adults? Calm your children. All it is is eternal rest."

He turned the corner to view the front of the vehicle.

"Hold it!"

The voice punctured the relative silence like a gunshot.

Rayne froze.

A thin, short man with balding blonde hair and a snake-hide bandana held a massive antique rifle.

"Drop the walkin' stick and take off the bag. You got anything good?"

"I don't know? What do you consider good?"

"Well, for one, I'll go ahead and take them shoes. You got any booze or cigarettes. I'm gonna wanna celebrate."

"No cigs, no booze. Maybe a can of beans or two. Mostly clothes and bedding."

"Take off the bags, boy."

Rayne turned a quarter of an inch to get a better look at the hermit robbing him. He looked particularly bizarre in the tattered rags of what clearly used to be a Scout Master's uniform.

"Come on give me your shit."

Rayne shook his head.

"Not a chance in hell, old man. Shoot me."

"That's how it's gonna be?"

"You're gonna have to become a murderer today if you're gonna be a thief. I'd rather die than spend a day out here without my shit. Last person to try to steal from me is floating at the bottom of a river."

"You can't float at the bottom of a river, dumbass. You got a goddamn mouth and a confidence you didn't earn," the old man said. "See how strong you sound now."

The haggard mountain man fired the rifle and shattered Rayne's hand. Unseen birds fluttered out of the brambles as the rifle shot resounded through the hills. The bullet hadn't struck his palm dead center. It ended up grazing the tips of his fingers, but the momentum of the high caliber round was enough to pull his hand apart.

He screamed uncontrollably and cried like a child. His throat was raw within the first few seconds of screaming. His knees buckled and he raised his trembling forearm to see what was left of his ring finger which dangled by a strip of connective tissue.

His attacker set the rifle against the grill of the truck, presumably to conserve bullets. He stepped before Rayne as he pulled a large buck knife from his belt.

Rayne was paralyzed by fear and pain. He simply cried as the mountain scavenger stood over him, letting his tears and snot drip onto the ground.

The man first cut the straps to his pack and lifted it off of Rayne, then grabbed his wrist and sliced off the hanging finger.

Rayne failed to struggle his mangled hand free.

"Look like tender meat to me," the old man said, smiling. He forced the hand close to his lips and took a deliberate bite, sucking at the blood, pulling at the exposed bone fragment.

Rayne uttered a shrill, animalistic scream, writhing and kicking from the pain.

He finally let go wiping the blood from his beard.

"You taste 'bout as good as stainless steel, but I bet you got an ass as soft as hog meat."

Rayne began to crawl away on his back when he heard a terrifying, familiar noise from the brush: the near-silent mechanical report of lost tension; a cord being let loose. An arrow materialized in the center of the old man's stomach. He almost didn't react. He just looked down at his stomach as if studying the arrow alone would heal him.

The hunter with the disfigured, inhuman face approached from behind the rhododendrons. It had been tracking him. The hunter took out its own knife and severed the tendons in the old man's knees. He dropped to the ground and the hunter pressed its boot against his skull. The man's expression of anguish collapsed. His eyes reddened and separated as they bulged from their sockets and his clenched yellowing teeth cracked and folded into one another as the gums split. Before Rayne's eyes, his head was flattened.

Seeing the small opportunity, his will to live was invigorated. He rolled over to the fire and grabbed the enamel pot of coffee, dumping it. The stew pot tipped over as well, dousing the flames further, kicking up an immense plume of steam and carbon dust. He was hidden for a moment and used the cloud of steam to slip behind the wide trunk behind the beaver carcass. He had a narrow vantage point and watched as the steam settled.

He stopped thinking. Whatever strategic faculties he had at his disposal, any innovative thoughts he could exploit, were gone, completely exhausted. His gut churned as if it were filled with molasses. His shaky legs carried him forward. Running was all he had. An arrow landed hard into the center of a hickory trunk. The next sailed along till it lost momentum. He zig-zagged around the trees for cover, running as fast as possible, nearly unable to catch a breath. His lungs stung. He tripped over a root and scrambled behind a rock, his ankles beginning to swell. He kept going, limping across the dead leaves. There was no incline or drop off this time. The forest kept going. He had reached a plateau. The disfigured hunter on his trail never gave up. Rayne could feel the size of his ankle growing in his boot. He clenched his wounded hand.

The sun was out in full. He saw a thicket of blackberry bushes ahead, thorny desiccated stalks killed off in the frost overnight. He limped toward them for cover. He realized then, that his hand was still bleeding profusely. The blood had dripped down his shirt and pants in a bright red crust. He saw spots as he blinked and struggled to focus his eyes on the hunter. Beyond the bramble patch, he finally saw a dirt road: two thick grooves in the soil where nothing had the time to grow; a makeshift thoroughfare blazed by daily tire tread. And in his delirium, he believed he saw an old pickup truck barreling down the rugged pathway. He crawled across the dead leaves and waved down the vintage Chevy with his good hand. The pickup came to a stop, but the driver kept the engine running and the windows rolled. Rayne approached the vehicle in hysterics, smearing blood on the passenger's side window. The arrows started flying, glancing off the solid metal chassis. Rayne dove into the bed of the truck, wedging himself inside the load of firewood and coiled copper line. He felt the Chevy slope to one side as the arrows struck the tires. An arrow cracked the glass on the passengers window. The old man had already slid out of the driver's seat, ducking for cover behind the truck. He had taken a long pump-action shotgun from beneath his seat and a gray revolver from his overall pocket. Rayne covered his ear as best he could as the driver rested the stock of the shotgun against the truck bed, the barrel only inches from Rayne's face, as he shot back at the hunter. They traded fire for a few minutes, then the old man abandoned the shotgun, took out the pistol, squinted, held his breath, then fired four times.

He exhaled and tossed the hot pistol on the wheel frame.

"I got'em," he said

Rayne peaked over the firewood.

"You're sure?"

"Yeah, he's down."

"You're a hundred percent?"

The bearded man handed him the grip of the pistol.

"You wanna walk up there and plant one more in his skull to make you feel better?"

Rayne shook his head.

"Didn't think so. Now, get the hell out of the truck."

"Take me to a hospital," Rayne said, showing him his hand.

The old man took out an oil blotched rag for a tourniquet and wrapped it painfully tight around his wrist.

"You ain't gonna make it to a hospital in time, you're already white as a ghost."

The old man hoisted Rayne out the truck bed and let him fall to the dirt.

"You're lucky though. I got a friend who should be coming down the road now. He can fix you up."

"What?"

"Just wait here. He's not far behind."

Rayne tried to speak but found himself barely able.

"Cellphone?"

"Do I look like I got a cellphone?"

Rayne vomited stomach acid and began to ramble incoherently. He looked out at the treeline where the road curved and saw Jac's white van, then passed out.

13

There had been this one road (if he could think of it that way) in Nebraska flanked on each side by a long sweep of flora, some bulbous honeysuckle-hued cash crop with no name. The tractor's path went on into eternity as he passed tin sheds, barn homes, and teetering rooster-shaped weather vanes. He could see at least half a mile ahead. The sky directly above him was a cloudless dark blue, bluer than the swimming pool he had stared at in a neighbor's backyard when he first tried acid the previous spring. That neighbor had been a good friend, and introduced a lot of the local high school kids to vinyl records and the virtues of the tube amp. People used to lie about Spookrat having played a set on his patio once. He had probably started the rumor himself. Kids used to call him Jerry because he looked like the guy from The Grateful Dead. His real name was Ben, or Ken. Rayne got most of his weed and Triple Cs from Jerry, who in turn had gotten most of his stuff wholesale from a black guy everyone called Wolfman. His acid carried his signature on the blotter paper--a detailed sepia still of Lon Chaney Jr in full wolf mask. It was like letting a commemorative stamp dissolve on your tongue. He had stared at the pool for two hours, and never saw anything so goddamned blue in his life. Now, fully sober, he saw the same shade of blue overhead.

In the distance, to the northeast, where he could see far enough ahead it was like looking into the future, the sky went dark and, after a few minutes of walking, everything before him grew hazy as the wall of rain moved in, watering the crops. The heat was instantly replaced by a strong cooling wind that whipped the fields as if the world were undulating. Omaha was still a ways. He put on his poncho and took out a little piece of jerky and ate it, then took half a salvaged Marlboro from his pouch and lit it with a match. He smoked it down beneath the hood of the poncho. He fantasized about finding a cornfield where he could eat as much as he liked and maybe run into a loose farmgirl with whom to spend the night.

By the time the rain stopped, the unidentifiable flowers gave way, finally, to some corn. But it had just been planted. Ankle-high tufts of green reached out of the wet soil.

A few more cycles of rain and sunshine moved over the tilted land before the night set in like a swathe of purple linen tossed over the now endless fields of okra-colored leaves. The dirt on either side of the road had been freshly tilled and the ripples in the modified terrain looked like wrinkled carpet rolled out across the earth.

He was dry by the time he could no longer see his hand in front of him. He didn't dare stop and set a fire. The last thing he needed was some shotgun-wielding farmer accusing him of attempting to burn down his barn.

Eventually the little blaze of the road led to a proper freeway. The signs were illegible in the full dark. He wasted another Diamond brand Walmart match to elicit the green glare of the state highway sign.

The sign read, "FORT LARAMIE 198 miles."

He had been going the wrong way. Omaha was an entire continent away from him at this point. He needed a city; a place with trash cans and discarded half coffees tossed away by careless yuppie scumbags, where other traveling kids could pool their resources and go in for an 18-pack at a local gas stop, where people walking the streets had loose dollars to spare, where abandoned industrial parks were full of discarded hospital-room cots and empty metallic drums ready for a warming fire. The road to Wyoming would sap his supplies in four days maximum. He considered, for the first time in his travels, hitching a ride. Hitchhiking was not typical for most crust punks. Their haggard image made them look too dangerous to stick out their thumbs on the open road for most passerbys, and too tempting an opportunity for roaming sadists who might want to cut them off. But his options were limited.

He walked down the Nebraska interstate and stuck out his thumb or just waved erratically to each floating couplet of orb-shaped light gliding across the still, rainslick asphalt. It wasn't long after, a drunk cowboy stopped for him. He had a Ram truck and inside a cooler of Buds and a knockoff whiskey bottle jammed into the cupholder.

"You on drugs, boy?"

"No," he said.

"You know how to drive?"

"I got an Ohio state license, yessir."

"I'll give you fifty bucks to drive me home," he said, almost like a question.

"Let's see the money."

The cowboy reached into his jeans like he was scratching his crotch and pulled out a calfskin wallet chained to his belt loop. He gave Rayne a crisp twenty dollar bill.

"That's not fifty."

"Half now and half when I get there."

"That's not even half."

"God damn it! You want it or not?"

"Alright."

They switched seats, walking around the grill of the truck. The cowboy staggered.

He drove him about eight miles down the road in silence. The cowboy popped the glove compartment to the truck. Rayne watched him, taking note of where he had his apple knife. He imagined the flicking it open and slicing the guy's throat. The cowboy wasn't reaching for a gun. He took out a bottle of children's electrolyte formula and began to chug it.

"I haven't had a hangover in years," he said, wiping his lips.

Rayne said nothing.

"So how come you're homeless?"

"I'm traveling. This is a personal choice. I'm on a spiritual journey."

"You got nowhere to go?"

"Not at the moment."

"Then you're fuckin' homeless. How come you left home?"

Rayne shrugged.

"You're daddy didn't like it that you're gay?"

"I'm not gay."

"That's a shame," the cowboy said and stroked Rayne's cheek with the back of his hand.

"I'm fifteen," he lied. "You're sure you want to risk going to jail?"

"Let me see that driver's license."

"What?"

"The one from Ohio you said you had. I wanna see it, god damn it."

"I'm driving your truck. I can't just reach in and grab it."

"Well, then. Let me help you."

He reached over the Rayne pants.

Rayne slammed hard on the breaks.

The cowboy's head cracked against the dashboard.

"Ahh! You fucker."

Rayne took out the apple knife and stuck the cowboy's shoulder. The cowboy, numbed by the booze, went back for the glove compartment, rifling through papers.

He wasn't about to let him get a gun. He took the whiskey bottle, having seen the trick once in a movie, and swigged a mouthful, quickly spewing it into the drunk's eyes. It bought him enough time to put the truck in neutral, unbuckle the seat belt and jump out with his pack. He was used to jumping to and from moving surfaces and caught his balance quickly.

The truck careened into a gulch.

Rayne hid behind the highway median and watched as the cowboy, face and arm covered in blood, got back into the driver's seat and drove away. The front bumper was halfway off, grating a line of sparks down the highway like a bottle rocket.

14

He was sedated on good medical-grade dope, eyes wandering the room, soaking in the colors of a waking dream, moving from behind the curtains draped over the window sill....reflections of coveted daylight on fabric....and sudden darkness....

In the blink of an eye, the day was gone. A nurse, he figured it had been a nurse, must have walked into the room and opened the curtains to watch the rain. Perhaps she, he also assumed the nurse had been a woman, needed to see the parking lot to check on their car in the impending sleet and hail, or, and this was a longshot, they thought he might like to see the sunshine before nightfall, that was, presuming he woke up in time within his dope-induced semi-coma. There was a clock on the far end of the room. It was close to the two in the morning. Strange now, he thought, that he had a good sense of time and place, thinking relatively clear. His eyes followed the tube in his arm to the bag of IV fluid, then cased the dim, stuffy room. The walls were covered in drab green tile as if he were being looked after in a bathhouse; an old decorative scheme from the 1970s. His wound was dressed in a massive bundle of gauze; the thumb completely invisible while only the tips of his index and middle fingers jutted out the top of the woven bandage. The only light was a sliver of cold fluorescence from the lengthy echo chamber of the hospital corridor beaming through the square of reinforced glass in the center of the locked door.

He couldn't imagine a small town like Last Junction as the home of any kind of in-patient facility like this one. It had to be a regional hospital somewhere close to a Catholic diocese judging from the cross mounted to the tile above his pillow. He might be as far out as Chattanooga, Tennessee by now with any luck, he thought.

He stood up from his cot, figuring he had rested enough and would do some unwanted roaming around the halls until an orderly or security guard stopped him. He dragged his IV stand with him as he carefully opened the heavy door. Someone had taken a knife or screwdriver and carved the letters 'GWY' into the dark grain of the wood.

The hall was peaceful. The mounted clock ticked like the chirp of an unseen grasshopper. The light was irritating, causing him to squint. The fluorescent tubes overhead made an unusual hum; a consistent murmur that effectively dulled any thought.

He stepped down the wide corridor with the IV stand and turned at one of the elevators. The second walkway led him to an open air lobby. He sat down in a plush coffee table chair and propped his feet up on a rolling ottoman. His attention turned to the vending machine in the far corner as a full bottle of Mountain Dew fell out the open port and rolled across the floor. The bottle stopped in the center of the rug, its label facing him. He stood up from the chair and gripped the IV stand, staring where the vending machine continued to produce a strange pneumatic hissing as if it were a boiler in some overheated basement. He set his foot on the rolling ottoman and kicked it over to the bottle, hiding it from his line of sight. The rollers didn't get far on the carpet. He pulled the stand closer and walked away into a brighter hall. He was searching for a water fountain. He found one close to an empty check-in desk. Making sure no nurse or night shift employee would see him, he crept toward the stainless steel fountain and knelt down to take a drink. The water pressure was low and he had to crouch down almost sucking the water from the nozzle. There was a distant squeaking of wheels and he thought and orderly or janitor might be coming down the hall. He wiped his face of excess water and ducked behind a protruding section of wall close to the fountain. Peering around the corner, he watched as the ottoman rolled down the hall knocking into the side of the drinking fountain before gliding back into the hallway where it stopped.

"Nope," he said out loud. "Not like this."

He repeated the mantra as he shuffled away, letting the bag of intravenous fluid swing back and forth on the metallic hook. The needle was heavy in the crook of his arm. He didn't know what was in the translucent pouch; dope, saline, electrolytes. The last time he went to a doctor, he was six. He wasn't sure how much he needed whatever it was dripping into his veins, slowing him down. He ripped out the needle and put pressure on the pinprick of blood as it dripped down his forearm. He found an elevator and pressed the button on the wall. The doors parted immediately. The interior was musty just like the room; the odor of old wood. He got to the bottom floor and stepped into the hallway still cradling his arm.

The lights were somewhat weaker the closer he got to the entrance, or one of the many entrances. The fluorescents here altered the hue of his bandage from white to a pale, neon green. He could see automatic doors ahead near the emergency room desk, which also appeared vacant. He wiped some semi-coagulated blood off where the rust-colored iodine had been swabbed. It looked brighter in the strange new light, like tarnished gold.

He realized he was practically naked if it weren't for the hospital gown.

Where the hell was he supposed to find his clothes?

The cold from the icy rain outside showering the near empty parking lot seeped through the gaps in the automatic doors. He walked to the front desk and looked over at the computer monitor and empty chairs, then hoisted himself over the barrier, sneaking into the unlocked employee lounge. He put on some loose scrubs which had been neatly bundled and placed in a pile inside several cloth laundry baskets and tied the draw strings as best he could with one hand. He still had some feeling in the tips of the fingers sticking out from the miles of bandages. If he got to keep his thumb, there was still hope to one day learn to play the bass guitar. He drank more water from a paper cone and gallon jug—the kind he had only seen on TV—and searched the coat closet and open lockers for anything that he might use as shoes. There was a crusty pair of women's tennis shoes in one locker, but they were barely large enough for him to slip in his toes. Beneath a navy blue peacoat on a hanger stood a pair of dark rubber galoshes. It was the best fit he could find. He doubled up on someone's dirty socks to keep his feet warm and to prevent them from swimming in the large rubber boots. He cracked open the door to check for anyone who might have caught him stealing, then, once he saw he was still alone, stepped into the rectangular barrier of the front desk, pulling on the navy blue peacoat. He felt the pockets for any personal items, but found only a sandwich receipt.

He looked to his right and nearly collapsed.

Catching his breath on the floor, he sat upright, hiding behind the walls of the desk, trying to process what he saw standing in the lot just beyond the glass; some creature with a bulbous head and snake-like body.

He looked back over the stacked envelopes and was relieved. It was no creature, just a darkly complected man wearing a turban and a long, heavy winter coat. Streaks of jet black hair stuck through the portions of the wrap which looked to be a different style than the religious pagh he was used to. The wind had most likely blown it apart. The man appeared to have a reflector on a lanyard, catching the light from the emergency room sign.

Rayne allowed his heart rate to stabilize and crawled over the desk to talk to the first person he had seen all night. The automatic doors parted slowly. He approached, hoping he was a doctor, fully aware that he might recognize the stolen coat.

"Hi, you work here?"

The man said nothing, but made eye contact with him.

Rayne noticed the reflector on his necklace was actually a medallion of silver.

"Do you speak English?"

He noticed the man had buckles on his shoes.

"Sorry, I thought you were a doctor or something."

The man continued to stare, smiling at him without speaking.

The turban material looked heavy, woolen. It was not a Dastaar, and the mute man didn't appear to be Sikh. His outer jacket looked more like a cape, something Jack the Ripper might have worn on the dark streets of England.

He extended his hand, offering something to Rayne.

Rayne reached out to take whatever he had.

The man placed what looked like a dry piece of tree bark in his palm. He held it for a moment and smelled it. It was a twist of pure tobacco. He looked up from his hand and the man was gone.

15

His first spiritual experience.

He looked through the brush and evergreens surrounding the lot.

Nothing.

He thought of the girl in the derelict church. He stood alone in the street.

Communing with ghosts.

He checked his pocket to make sure the tobacco hadn't vanished. It was still there, brittle and dry like a stale cigar.

He returned to the automatic doors and stepped through the threshold, treading silently down the hall, elevated, smiling to himself. It was as if he were being bolstered by an unseen force, his steps requiring no effort.

As soon as it began, the feeling was squashed and the weight equal to an extra human being pushed him back to the floor.

He passed a small corridor leading to a fire exit where he saw another man, white, with a shaved head, wearing the same scrubs he had just stolen. The man paced under the exit sign. Blood soaked his lower abdomen and crotch.

Rayne hid behind the corner and watched him in a dim reflection on the glass guarding the extinguisher affixed to the opposite wall. He was tapping a butcher's knife against his forehead, lost in thought as he paced. He wasn't using the blunt edge. Each absent-minded tap left a significant cut. Blood trickled down his face.

"Fuckin' shit, man," he mumbled, pacing. "Enver Hoxha, fuckin' Nikolai Ceacesceau."

Rayne listened as the manic nurse spouted off the names of Eastern-European dictators. He didn't recognize most of the names, but the few he did gave him enough context.

"Pol Pot, Mao Zedong, Ho Chi Minh."

He was moving on to Asia. Blood trickled down his face and dripped audibly onto the buffed and waxed floor. He wiped his face and slammed the bloody handprint on the door. Rayne pressed his back against the wall, attempting to slowly push himself up. His heel slipped.

The squeak of rubber carried across the abandoned first floor.

He fell hard on his tailbone.

The wet slap of another bloody handprint.

Footfalls carried toward him.

His knees crunched as he stood.

The ring of the blade scratching against the wall.

He ran into the dark of a nearby lab, his face sweltering.

He could feel his cheeks flush. The blood drained from his fingertips, numbing them. He clenched his fist, trying to get some feeling back.

The blood-soaked nurse's footfalls were heavy and calculated, like the crack of an old metronome.

Rayne took shelter behind a cabinet and did what he could to control his breathing.

The nurse kicked open the door, plunging the knife into stacks of paper and folders, knocking over jars of cotton and gauze which shattered without echo. He sniffled, wiping his nose with the back of his hand still holding the wide kitchen blade. A noise from the hall caught his attention and he wandered away like an animal.

Rayne sighed.

His stomach churned.

From the cabinet door beside him, he heard a labored cough.

He hesitated before whispering, "Hey? Hey? Are you hiding in there?"

"Fuck off, kid. There ain't no more room."

"Have it your way," he said, pulling himself to his feet. He limped to the door and, carefully, looked past the hinges into the pale, green light of the hall.

A pair of scrub pants with gray tennis shoes twitched in a growing pool of black blood just past the corner. He watched as the body was dragged away, mopping along a heavy wave in the stinking puddle.

He remembered Dorn saying that people were just giant balloons full of blood while they had been watching something about construction accidents on TV.

He searched the room for anything he could use as a weapon.

Nothing.

Just the cotton balls and broken glass at his feet.

He opened the cabinet beneath the sink unit.

The hiding man had a gray moustache and wore a dark green maintenance-issued jumpsuit.

He pulled the door closed again.

"I told you to find your own spot."

"You got a knife on you?"

"No."

"Anything, man. I don't want in your spot. I just need a weapon."

After a short delay of hesitation, the cabinet door cracked ajar and the older man tossed out a textured-grip monkey wrench. He picked up the tool and stared at the grooved teeth of the open jaws. It was top heavy like a good club or a sap.

He stood in silence, strategizing with the wrench in his non-dominant hand.

Could he even hit him with his left?

He pictured himself trying to swing the wrench across the back of his skull only to graze his shoulder. He was no southpaw.

Accuracy was key with a weapon like that. You had to land in just the right spot to see your opponent go down in spasms, blood dripping from their ears; the kind of dead-on strike to keep them eating applesauce in their underalls in front of children's cartoons for the remainder of their life. Whatever it took, he didn't have it.

Gripping the handle tight, he crept down the opposite direction, making his way back to the ER doors.

He made it as far as the parking lot, before stalling. Crouched behind a row of frozen sticker shrubs, he took a mouthful of dirty ice from the green leaves and let it melt on his tongue. It was difficult to make out the terrain ahead of him as another cycle of hail swept through the mountain ranges. He was eventually able to see a gazebo in the field opposite the expansive lot. He ran across the blacktop past a wavering pine, over an icy curb. The field was littered with clods of cold-hardened red clay, strewn twigs, and loose brambles as sharp as razor wire. He trudged through, sliding in the rubber galoshes. The pants he had tied to his waist stuck to the back of his calves in the powerful gusts. He looked back to the entrance of the ER, now thirty feet away, and saw the bald man standing in the red light of the sign. He could see Rayne halfway to the gazebo. He knew he could. Through all the shadow and falling sleet, he could see him escaping to the field. He watched Rayne as he stared back and, slowly, amused, he lifted the severed head of the maintenance worker.

Rayne squinted and recognized the moustache.

When the nurse was done showing him his handiwork, he tossed the head across the pebbled walkway.

Despite what he assumed would happen, the severed head did not roll. It landed hard like a rock, never once rebounding.

The nurse stood in the cold, his breath visible as it billowed from his nostrils and open mouth like industrial smoke.

Rayne expected him to charge out into the field, but he returned to the warmth of the hospital, disappearing into the artificial lights, transforming into a distant silhouette.

Rayne collapsed onto the cold, dray wood of the gazebo floor. The cold would kill him. Even in the nurse's psychosis, he could see that if Rayne didn't find shelter within the hour he was a dead man, or so Rayne thought.

A blue body half immersed in ice.

He held himself as he shivered.

He was going to die here.

Back in Ohio, the cold used to take two or three homeless people each winter. They would down a bottle of bottom-shelf tanker-truck vodka and, while the neutral grain spirits were artificially warming them, doze off only to end up fused to the dying wood of an old park bench draped in a veil of white powder. He thought about the baby everyone at school had been talking about the year before he left, the year Trina, everyone's alleged first-time girl, got kicked out of her dad's house. Her dad still watched the three-month old most of the time while she was ringing bells and slinging eggs and hash at Mickey's Diner. He couldn't remember the child's name. Was it Christopher? Ryan?

On Christmas Eve, he took his granddaughter to his mother's eight miles northwest out of town so he could go drinking with his brother. Trina's grandmother was almost 90 and deep in the throes of the dementia that comes from a long life of doing nothing but what you were told to by men. The child ended up freezing to death, of course. The rumor was the grandmother had tossed him off the porch balcony and when she heard the cries, realizing what she had done, she couldn't find him. Her eyes and ears weren't what they used to be, and the snowfall was rapidly accruing over the backyard. She lost four fingers to frostbite before dying of pneumonia in the hospital. When the paramedics pulled Trina's son out of four feet of snow, he was blue and black and frozen solid. He thought of the old woman in that dark yard listening to the baby's muted screams as she tore her hands apart digging through snow and solid ice.

Rayne closed his eyes.

Two headlights blinked on and off in the distance. They briefly switched to brights which cast light over the field, then died.

He sat up and looked past the torrents to find their source.

They flashed again.

He had enough time to catch a glimpse of the white Chevy Astro parked on the opposite end of the hospital's ER doors. He ran toward the van thinking only of its warmth.

The sleet stung against his face.

He bashed the ice off the frozen passenger door handle.

The van was unlocked and he jumped inside, closing the door. Desperately breathing on his one uncovered hand, his head low in the collar of the stolen peacoat, Rayne looked around the empty van for Jac. He reached over to the driver's seat and flipped on the dash lights.

Behind him, buckled in the otherwise empty seat like a child, sat the wooden doll dressed like a lumberjack. The same dead blue eyes stared back at him.

He could hear breathing again; hiss-like, raspy breaths. He stared at the slight opening in the doll's nutcracker mouth as if the doll itself were breathing. But the noise of the breaths were familiar to him. The wrinkled sound of plastic carried with it. It was coming from behind the doll, in the very back of the van. He screwed with the outdated buttons of the old Chevy until the cabin lights flickered on and he saw four plastic bags again. The outlines of small hands, children's hands, worked the plastic from the inside, the black material conforming to their mouths and faces as they sucked for air.

There were no keys in the ignition, nor anywhere in the van. He ran out, leaving the door ajar, heading back to the hospital where he'd take his chances rather than freeze to death. The nurse with the butcher's knife was at least six corridors away. He entered the main lobby, thinking he could barricade himself in a room until sunup.

Bodies slashed and mutilated by the butcher's knife had been lined up against the elevator doors: a young blonde woman in scrubs, an elderly black man with graying hair, a doctor, his white coat soaked red at the bottom.

A bloody swastika had been painted on the wall. It was already starting to fade.

There had been talk of Nazi's on the road. They were more dangerous than cops.

The floor was covered in the nurse's bloody shoe prints; an erratic dance instructional. His own flat prints from the wet galoshes disrupted and smeared the half-coagulated imprints. He turned into a small dining hall.

The clatter of pots and pans sent him into another panic. The rustling came from beyond the closed aluminum roll-up window at the far end of the hall. There were stacks of clean trays and an empty garbage bin beside a slender door to the kitchen extension. He ducked beneath the table, hoping to blend into the darkness.

A tall man emerged from the kitchen door in winter gear and ski mask.

Rayne recognized the dark green raincoat. He carried a backpack sideways around his abdomen and wore fingerless bicycle gloves. On his back, he carried a lever-action rifle with a leather bandolier of six extra cartridges strapped to the stock as if he were some kind of militia fighter. He was stuffing packs of bacon, bean cans, and fresh green apples into the backpack. As he zipped the faded pack closed, the bald nurse kicked open the door.

"I will not be replaced!"

The man in the ski mask turned slightly and made eye contact with Rayne beneath the table.

Rayne raised his mound of bandages and spread open his left hand, asking not to be shot.

"Sich Heil!" the nurse raised the knife.

The man in the dark raincoat shifted the stance of his feet, bending his knees, placing one foot before the other, and pulled a small pistol from his open pocket. With both hands on the gun, he took a single shot and the nurse's neck bent backwards in an instantaneous, violent jerk. His face, already bloody, lost expression. A strange red mist lingered in the air like iron dust. He collapsed onto the floor and deep black blood began spilling from the back of his cracked skull.

He pointed the gun at Rayne, who begged him not to shoot again.

"Sorry, kid. You gotta get put down before you go bezerk on me."

"I'm not going to go crazy."

"You don't know it yet, but you will."

He lifted the ski mask above his face and brushed his long hair behind his ears. It was the young man Jac had called the Cherokee.

"I remember you. I even gave you a chance to turn back."

"Turn back from what? Don't fuckin' kill me."

"Sorry, man. It ain't nothin' personal."

Rayne reached into his pocket and took out the twist of tobacco.

"Does this mean anything?"

"What is that a dog turd?"

"It's tobacco. A ghost gave it to me."

"Put it on the ground."

Rayne dropped it.

"Slide it over. You see this little gun. This is a Sig Sauer number 238. Nice little pocket gun. You try shit… well… you've already seen what I can do with it."

He slid the twist to his feet. He knelt down and picked it up.

"Where did you get this?"

"A ghost."

"What did it look like?"

"What?"

"The ghost dumb-ass. What did it look like?"

"I don't fuckin' know."

He aimed the pistol between Rayne's eyes.

"You better plumb the depths of your memory or I'm gonna fuckin' shoot you."

"Okay, he had a silver medallion and a turban."

"Oh, fuckin' bullshit. You're lyin' straight out of a goddamn Trail of Tears textbook."

"I don't know what you're fuckin' talking about."

"Yes you do, white boy. Or else you wouldn't have shown me this piece of shit tobacco. I'll see you in hell."

"Eg havi mist mína tasku. Eg eri skædd. Far burtur."

He lifted the barrel of the gun toward the ceiling.

"Wait. What the fuck language is that?"

"It's Faroese. It's where I was born."

"What did you say?"

"I lost my pack. I'm injured. Just let me be. I think that's what I said."

"Where are Faroese people from. Like Sweden?"

"Close to Iceland."

"You're not American. You weren't born on this land."

"No."

He pocketed the gun.

"In that case, I believe you."

16

"You do something bad enough and that evil gets left over, like an infection that won't heal. This place, man, Last Junction. We'll never know what happened here since Americans wrote all the history books but it must've been the apex of the shit, you know what I'm sayin'? The 1800s. The Indian Removal Act. You ever learn about the Trail of Tears in school? That little wedge of a paragraph right below all that positive shit about the Revolutionary War and how great it was. Whatever happened here. It hypnotizes people. It sends them crazy. It's pure fuckin' evil."

"What is this some Native American burial ground curse?"

"That's a bunch of bullshit, man. It ain't ever our fault. Whatever shit fucks with people here, it wasn't left by us. It was left by y'all. White people, man. The colonists put some kind of ancient European pagan hoodoo on the land here to make sure no one else could have it. But it backfired on'em. Once every few years, everybody who's a descendant of a colonist loses their mind. That's the main factor. That's what my grandpa figured."

"I thought you said we'd never know what happened here?"

"Who knows the true history. I learned all this shit from my grandpa, and inherited his big tract of land when he passed. I've been living here for six years."

"Why do you stay?"

"I ain't got nowhere else to go," he said, cracking the truck window to toss out the cigarette. "But you, man. You were in the wrong place at the wrong time. You're lucky to be alive at least five times over."

He paused and scratched his nose.

"My name's Jesse. I'm a descendant of freedom fighter Ned Christie from Tahlequah, Oklahoma."

He offered his hand, keeping one on the steering wheel.

Rayne awkwardly shook it with his left.

"I'm Rayne."

"Don't give me your punk name. What's your real name? Do-desh-te-do-ah?"

"Dagur," he said. "My mom named me Dagur Aní Hemuðsen."

"Heh-Muth-Sen?"

"Hemuðsen."

"That's a cool fuckin' name. It's like a Viking name."

"It is a Viking name. What's your Cherokee name?"

"Jesse."

Rayne said nothing.

"I ain't got no Cherokee name. We all got normal names now in Oklahoma."

"Oklahoma?"

"Ah, man. I knew you didn't know shit. I gotta give you a history lesson. Trail of Tears survivors were forced to walk from here all the way to Oklahoma. Some folks stayed. They fought the system and holed up in the mountains. So now you got two nations. Eastern Band and Western Band. Kituwah and Otali. But a lot of folks got family on both sides. That's why I own the rights to the big chunk of land on the central slope hanging over Last Junction."

"Why don't you go back to Oklahoma where you're from? It's gotta be better than this crap. You wouldn't have to steal food from the hospital to eat out there, I'm sure."

"It's too dangerous to go grocery shopping or really any-where in town when people are like this. Why do you ride your rusty trains from city to city and beg on the street corner like the piece of shit?"

Rayne went silent for a moment.

"I guess I thought I was on some kind of spiritual journey."

"How's that working out for you?"

He showed him his bandaged hand.

"How does it look?"

"Living here ain't all bad. I got space and time to think. I don't have to do nothing I don't feel like and I ain't gotta listen to no manager or foreman. I do what I want when I want. I grow shit. I build shit. I fix old shit. I live. You know? I live in defi-ance of y'alls shit culture, ya'lls fucked up government. Every few years though, in early November, I hunker down and stay away from the main roads. That's when everybody loses it. Mother's throw newborns into ovens, cops start opening fire on people in the street, hunters stop going after deer."

"Then get me the fuck out of here."

"Where do you think I'm taking you now? We're headed to the county line."

"No," he said.

"The fuck I am. The best thing for you is to get out while you still can."

"I'm a street kid with nothing to my name but a hospital outfit and coat."

"Not my problem."

"Take me back to Cain's"

"He's not going to help you, Dagur. Matter fact, he's more dangerous than the rest."

"Yeah, but he's got a room full of backpacker's gear pretty close to the kitchen. I need supplies if I'm gonna get back on the road. Not to mention some real fuckin' shoes," he said, flapping the loose galoshes.

"I'm not helping you rob Cain."

"I'm not asking you to. Just get me there."

Jesse put another cigarette between his lips.

"It's your funeral," he said, lighting the end.

17

The windows of the cabin home were pitch black. The sheet-rock chimney looked damp and frigid, enclosed in a layer of jagged ice, smokeless against the night sky. Rayne couldn't smell anything besides the cigarette from Jesse's truck and the bracing scent of frost. Cain's palace now appeared to be less of a luxury lodge and more like an abandoned bunker where nature was fast reclaiming ownership.

Rayne had asked Jesse for a gun before he snuck inside. Cain was armed and likely to shoot, to which Jesse said, "You go first. I got your back."

"I thought you weren't helping me?"

"If I give you a gun, you're gonna blow your foot off. What are you gonna do with your hand bandaged like that. You're not a lefty."

"No," he said. "No, I'm not."

"You ever fired a gun?"

"A few days ago. Cain gave me his to try out."

"You charge ahead and I'll do the shooting if it comes to that. We're in and out in five minutes or else."

"Else what?"

"I walk."

They crouched down and ran across the driveway to the backyard. Jesse had the lever-action rifle drawn.

"We might have to break a window to get in," Rayne said.

"Check the doors first before you screw anything up."

Rayne carefully pulled back the screen door to the sunroom and patio. The screens were heavy with frozen moisture. He held it open for Jesse and carefully let the door retract into its frame, trying not to let the rusted spring creak. He felt the doorknob to the kitchen.

It was open.

They stepped inside the relative warmth of the kitchen. Rayne scanned the room before finding the door with the pile of discarded gear. He looked back the island in the kitchen and watched Jesse grab a ripe banana from the fruit bowl and eat silently. Inside the closet there was a single light bulb hanging from the wall and a little chain dangling past the glass of the archaic 40-watt. He pulled the chain and turned on the dim light.

"What the fuck are you doing?" Jesse whispered.

"I gotta see if the shit fits me before I steal it."

"Find some shit and then turn it off."

He searched frantically through everyone's shit. Slipping out of the galoshes, he first forced on some patched jeans, then looped a sturdy woven belt around his waist. He took out the tall pack, the one that had a bed roll and even a foam matt to go beneath. There were a pair of hefty tan hiking boots dangling from the top, the laces tied onto the thick zipper. He couldn't believe his luck. They fit like he had bought them in a store.

"Ho-ly shit!" he whispered under his breath. From that moment on, he had found the pack he was taking. He opened it up and took a quick inventory of the clothes: rain pants, a pocket knife, thick brown overalls, a fresh pack of store-bought underwear and socks, unused glowsticks, waterproof maps of the Appalachian Trail. This wasn't the pack of a crust punk. He checked the zippers and found a wallet. Inside was a hundred-dollar bill American, an assortment of cards--credit and the like--and a college issued ID. The name read "Paul De Bakker." The faded image of a smiling blonde kid in his early twenties looked back at him. He looked further and found a red passport that said, "Koninkrijk Der Nederlanden: Paspoort." He took one of the fleece over-shirts made to look like flannel with the red checker pattern and breast pockets on the outside and a gray interior that was soft to the touch and pulled it over his scrub shirt. Both were loose on his withered frame.

"Get a move on," Jesse whispered.

He discarded the passport and the wallet, but kept the hundred dollars and the college I.D.

"Let's get the fuck out of here."

They didn't bother to stay quiet as they ran into the cold, letting the screen door slam behind them. He looked back at the bay windows above the garage where he had jumped days before.

They got back inside Jesse's truck and drove around a dark bend into the forest.

18

On the way to the county line, Jesse gave Rayne a pack of waterproof matches as well as an apple and a can of corned beef.

"For your travels," he said.

"I appreciate it. Can I have that tobacco back?"

"No," he said. "I'm keeping that. It's right that I'm keeping that."

Rayne said nothing.

Jesse glanced at him, then returned his attention to the dark mountain road.

"I lied about my name earlier."

"Yeah?"

"I have a Cherokee name."

"Yeah?"

"O-hee-sow-DAH-nay-huh."

"That means Jesse?"

"No. My grandpa gave it to me. It means lonesome."

"Fitting, I guess."

"So, Dagur. Why do you call yourself Rayne?"

"I thought it sounded cool. I thought it sounded suave in a street-smart way and chicks might like it."

Jesse took out a cigarette and set it between his lips. He thumbed the wheel of the lighter for a moment, thinking, before igniting the flame.

"Well, my grandpa named me 'lonesome' because he, unlike my mom and my aunt, saw who I was, who I was becoming. He knew I was better on my own. That's why he gave me and no one else the land. He gave me a place to be who I am. Everybody always talks about evil in really weird terms. The English language metaphor is always darkness. You know, an evil comes along and it brings the dark. When somebody's life turns for the worse, that person has gone to a dark place. I think dark places are good, man. A wounded animal retreats into the darkness to suck its wounds and rest. Darkness is necessary. Darkness is recuperation. I ain't sayin' I got anything against the light either. But light is a different way of looking at the world. Some of us are born to the dark and other's to the light, and evil doesn't discriminate between the two."

Jesse was a lot like some of the alpha-types he knew from the rails. Loners who'd dictate their manifestos once they figured you were listening. Even if he didn't like what Jesse had to say, the kid, he figured he must have been no older than his mid-twenties, had saved his life.

Jesse slowed the truck to a roll, letting the tires squash the debris into the icy mud, then pulled around to an outcrop of gray rocks shrouded in dying rhododendrons. The peculiar leaves had turned mostly yellow with flecks of black. They looked like ripe bananas in the truck's lights.

Jesse pointed up through the windshield and said, "Past that rock up yonder is an old iron bridge and on the other side of that, you're in Tennessee."

"Free and clear?"

"Far as I know."

"I hope I never come back," Rayne said.

"I hope you never do either."

He opened the passenger door and jumped out into the cold. He tossed his gear across his back, slammed the door shut then moved around to the front of the truck to give Jesse a thumbs-up with his left hand, and one last look. Moisture spiraled like smoke in the headlights.

Jesse waited for him to scale the rock and see the outline of the walking bridge against the dark blue of the infant dawn before driving away.

Rayne could barely see in front of him. The night was still thick on the earth while the first beams of morning were beginning to rip the sky apart. He held tight to the railing and stepped forward, staring upward at the silhouette of the iron beams as if he were walking through the ribcage of some giant animal, each footfall echoing.

He could hear the creek below.

It sounded distant; a fatal plummet between the creaky floor of the bridge and the jagged rocks. He couldn't see anything over the railing, just a black abyss where the rain disappeared. He was careful and strategic when he shifted his weight in case a waterlogged, ice-covered beam were to snap beneath him. He tucked his bandaged arm into the right sleeve of the peacoat to keep it dry. It was strange walking on the left side of the precarious structure, knowing that he would have chosen the opposite end if he hadn't been shot. Perhaps his injury had spared him from the path of a flimsy board or a patch of loose nails, but he doubted it. Nothing happened for a reason. He needed his hand looked at once he found a hospital in Tennessee. He was sure the wound needed to be tended further in one way or another. The hundred-dollar bill would probably go to waste on that alone. He'd try not to pay if he could get away with it.

The railing ended and the boards underfoot turned to mud and pebbles. He stepped along a hiker's trail and pushed his way through some startlingly visible ferns and rhododendrons. They were glowing alone in the forest, which filled him with an insurmountable dread.

He stopped to search the stolen pack's inventory. He found a wool cap and stretched it over his wet hair.

He followed the trail to the edge of a chainlink fence. He found the gap and passed through near a rusted frisbee goal. The dirt trail became paved in a pebbled concrete. There were green benches between a tennis court and a derelict playground with broken swings and a frozen metal slide. The court was lit up by the kind of stadium lights he had seen in his smalltown high school. It was a bad place for a park; domestic life encroaching on the wild.

He sat down on the bench after wiping the seat dry with his sleeve then took out his pack and looked through more of the Dutch backpacker's things. He hoped he had missed something like a larger knife or a pouch of tobacco with rolling papers, but he had gotten a good grasp of everything he carried. He zipped up his pack, looked off into the distance.

The rain stopped and morning set in across the sky. He could see beyond the stadium lights past the park where the trees parted. A long, white plume of smoke dissipated toward the drab clouds. He could tell from experience the fire was unregulated, an open campfire. The smoke trail was too wide and too easily influenced by the wind to be chimney smoke.

He checked the Dutch hiker's multitool. The flat blade was short. The toothed saw blade was significantly sharper from lack of use, but it had no tip. He couldn't stab with it, only slash. He took out a small pair of binoculars and looked out at the smoke. There wasn't much else to see from his current position. He moved toward the edge of the park.

There was a good spot near the chainlink on a hill. He surveyed the small valley beneath him to find the source of the fire. Crouching behind the cover of the grass on the hill, he watched the smoke until the morning finally displaced the dawn halflight. The world was visible again even beneath the heavy cloud cover. He stashed away the binoculars and took his chances walking toward the campfire.

A thin asphalt road came into view. Not a municipal thoroughfare, but the kind of narrow path built for a golf course. It looked odd the way it snaked out from the treeline and bisected the empty field. Parked just off to the side was a red Jeep trailing a pop-up camper.

He kept his distance.

A family of four sat around the campfire in folding chairs. The young woman cooked over a tripod while the father picked at a beige guitar. The two children were still draped in green blankets and looked to be half asleep in their chairs. Everything they had looked new as if it were still on display in a department store. The chairs had tags on them and the tripod grille wasn't yet completely blackened by the flames.

He moved along the little road past them, choosing not to make eye contact. They waved at him anyway.

"Good morning," the woman said over the fire. She had an Eastern European accent.

"Good morning," he said, looking up.

The father set the guitar down, propped it against the the tire of the jeep. He turned around in his folding chair to get a look at the stranger.

"You hiking?"

"I'm passing through, on to the next town."

"Where did you come up from?"

"Asheville," he lied.

"Oh, so you're going west. Trying to hike Nantahala or Chattahoochee?"

"Actually, I was looking for a town."

"Well, you're not going to find anything that way. We just took the kids through the Great Smokies. We're gonna dip down to Sylva, North Carolina and spend some time with an associate ministry before driving back to Virginia."

"I guess Knoxville is my next logical stop."

The young man whistled.

"Well, good thing you got your camping gear 'cause Knoxville's a ways on foot."

"If I go back this way on the road, where will that take me?"

"This funny little road here? It meets up with another back road that runs all the way to the NC border around the Cherokee Reservation."

"We just came from the museum about a day ago after getting back from the smokies," the young woman said flipping a pile of yellow eggs.

"You walked all this way from Asheville?" the father said.

"Just about."

"What happened to your hand?" she said, plating the eggs.

"It's a long story."

"If you're headed out for a long, long hike to Knoxville, you better conserve your resources. Would you like some breakfast. We have more than we need and our kids never finish anything."

"That's very kind…"

"Did you wrap your hand up yourself?" she said.

"No, I had it done in a hospital after I hurt it."

"Here, have a seat."

The father pulled out a folding chair from the back of the truck.

Rayne wanted to eat their eggs, but he was still too close to Last Junction to be at ease.

He sat down politely and took a plate. The young woman rousted the children out of their semi-sleep and gave them their food.

"Sausages?" the kid said.

"I haven't made sausages yet, Ben."

The father got their attention and introduced Rayne.

"Kids, this is…what's your name?"

"Dagur."

"This is Dagur. He's hiking the trail. And this is Ben and Ava. My name is Leslie and this is my wife Katja."

"Dagur?" Katja said, "Where is this name from?"

"I was born in the Faroes, but I'm from Ohio."

"I'm from Ukraine," she said. "I met Leslie while he was on mission."

The little girl looked at her father.

"Pharoh like in Egypt?"

"No, Ava. It's like.." he turned to Rayne. "The Faroe Islands are in the south pacific, right?"

"No," Katja said. "It's above the UK in the arctic."

Rayne nodded.

"I grew up in south Ohio," he said.

"But you have the wandering spirit of your ancestors: the Irish monks and Vikings who forged their way onto the islands," Katja said.

"I guess that's where it comes from."

The scrambled eggs, still steaming in the frigid morning ether, had deep orange yolks. It struck Rayne as a hassle to carry eggs on a camping trip. They must have purchased them in town. She set a long row of rich sausage links on the iron. They smelled of sage, maple syrup and brown sugar. The quality of their food must have been the foreign wife's decision. The father struck Rayne as a Wonderbread and baloney type. He had wished his own mother had put her foot down and kept on with the Scandinavian tradition of rye crips and smoked salmon, sheep bladder and whole cream, but Dorn would never part with his cube steak and French fries.

Rayne poked at his eggs, blowing on each piece.

He noticed they hadn't said grace. With food with on his plate, he wasn't in a position to question anything.

"Do you eat meat, Dagur?" she said.

"Of course," he said, watching the sausages sizzle as the grating beneath the iron swung over the fire. "That's a nice skillet."

"It puts more iron in the food. Good for the blood."

"It's hard to clean on the road, though," Leslie said.

"So, you mentioned ministry. What do you all do?"

"I'm a pastor," he said.

Rayne said nothing.

"You're not religious are you?"

"I'm not."

"And yet I sense something acutely monastic about you, Dagur," he said, spearing at the eggs with his fork. "You're searching for something aren't you?"

"I'm not looking for anybody."

"I didn't say that. You're on a journey aren't you?"

"I am."

"How's that been?"

"It was pretty awesome until the last town I just got through."

"Asheville?"

"Word to the wise," he said, alternating his gaze between Katja and Leslie. "Don't go just over the county line there. It's a crazy town."

"Where is it?"

"If you're trying to go back into North Carolina. Just drive around Last Junction."

Leslie got out his phone and scrolled to his GPS.

"You said…"

"Last Junction, North Carolina."

Leslie fiddled with his phone.

"There's nothing back that way but the Pisgah National Forest."

"Oh, it's there. It's a rough town. It's dangerous. Don't take your kids there."

"I don't see it. There's a town in Nevada called Scotty's Junction."

Rayne shrugged.

"Maybe, it's better that way. Nobody needs to find it," he said, smiling.

Leslie put away his phone and Katja began to plate the sausages.

Rayne kept smiling to himself.

19

The couple had given him a pocket bible, which he planned on using for toilet paper and rolling cigarettes. He spent the day in the forest, hiking along a trail Leslie had suggested. He moved slow and stretched his legs. There were no more random strangers. He gathered dry pieces of wood and set them in his pack to build a fire once the sun went down.

He ate his apple before he made the fire. He didn't sleep, keeping one eye open at all times, but rested until sunup. The morning was just as gray as the last. He made a tight roll of a page of deuteronomy, licked it shut, and lit the end on a hot coal from the fire. It was just paper, but it still felt nice to smoke. The sleeping bag was pulled down just below his chest and his arms were free, his head propped up on the pack. He watched the gray flakes of carbon peel away from the tip of the improvised cigarette.

20

Days later, he discovered a narrow logging road where the forest had been razed. His boots sank deep into the mud, so, when possible, he balanced himself on the stray logs and gridded joists of unwanted timber near the edge of the way. He followed the logging road for what he thought was close to an hour, though his concept of time was still fairly naive. In terms of distance, he might have traveled a mile by the time he found the work site. The team was long gone and everything was still. Mud and red clay caked the metallic tread of the backhoe. Flecks of chipped bark and green needles stuck to the grisly claws of the knuckleboom loader. He passed the foreman's trailer beside a shallow gulch. The scent of pine coalesced with the copper-like odor of the soil and frost. The piles of logs looked to him like the beginnings of a colonial era fortress.

He entered a valley of downed trees and heard the blare of a locomotive. He could see the tracks at the end of the valley, propped up by a short ridge. He was careful not to race across the trees. A branch could catch his foot and, if he fell forward, snap his ankle. The train had not yet approached the bend in the track where it passed the logging site. He came to the ridge and hid behind a fern.

The train was moving fast. He jumped out from the fern and counted the lug nuts on the wheels. He chose an open boxcar headed down the line and a stable mound of gravel close to the track where he could launch himself up to the ladder. Once those two points came within a foot of each other, he'd have one second to hit the mark, or else tuck in his legs and fall backward. He had never done it with only one good hand.

He took a deep breath.

The boxcar approached.

He jumped.

Rayne grabbed on with his left hand. The train's speed nearly pulled his arm out of his socket. He dangled for only a moment until, carefully, he landed his boots on the bottom rung of the ladder. When hanging freely, he tucked in his legs to protect them from the wheels. Some extended them and began flailing if they couldn't immediately find footing, which got a lot of kids sucked into the wheels.

He hopped inside the boxcar and sat against a pallet of wooden beams. He kept his foot on the edge of the car door and let the searing wind whip at his cheeks as he watched the foliage rush by. He started waxing poetic, talking to himself in verse about freedom and survival.

He felt so good, he wasted a match to light another fake bible cigarette and kept it burning in the side of his mouth like some turn-of-the-last century hobo.

The train continued through the forest, passing immense boulders and cliffs.

After an hour of riding, exhausted from lack of sleep, he closed the boxcar door, lay his head down and closed his eyes.

21

He was startled awake by a rush of Appalachian light and the grinding of metal. He sat up, but it was too late to hide. The railroad bull, an overweight man in a white uniform, had opened the boxcar door and was shining a flashlight into his eyes.

"Alright, get out."

"Let me get my bag, man."

"I said 'get out.'"

He pulled at Rayne's pant leg.

"Let me get my bag."

"I didn't tell you to get your bag. I told you to get out."

Rayne stood up in the boxcar. He was five feet higher than the guard on the ground. He threw on his pack and took his time buckling the straps.

"I don't go anywhere without my shit."

"GET DOWN!"

The bull screamed with enough exasperation his voice gave out.

Rayne jumped over the bull's head. It wasn't dark outside yet, but the drab skies were growing dim. The train had stopped almost halfway past an iron bridge that overlooked a river swollen with days of rain and ice. He took another step forward, away from the tracks, and, as he turned back to the bull, something heavy and black dominated his periphery.

The flashlight struck the back of his head. The bull then gave him a good kick and he fell headfirst into the uprooted reeds and tough clay, rolling with his pack down the incline to the edge of the riverbank below the tracks. The bull yelled something as he fell, but Rayne didn't hear it.

He didn't get up at first. With one eye open, he lay in the dust by the edge of the water. He could hear the door of the boxcar being shut; the distant crank muffled by the babbling over the nearby rocks.

He waited a long time. The bull never came down the slope to finish the job. Perhaps Rayne was too far from the railroad track to be in his jurisdiction. Once the train started to lurch forward, Rayne sat up and patted the loose reeds and red dust from his coat. He had a knot where the flashlight hit him, but he wasn't bleeding. He got back on his feet and walked directly beneath the cover of the bridge. The shadows flickered around him as the train picked up speed; the last beams of daylight breaking through the gaps between the passing compartments.

He exhaled, his breath thick.

Among the dirt was a rusted fifty-gallon drum lined with black soot halfway between the foundation and the river. It was as cold and stale as everything else beneath the bridge. There was also a stereo with an eight-track player caked in frost and mud beside a metal girder.

He recognized this place.

His eyes filled with tears he followed the empty cans of beer everyone had tossed away before they left him that morning to the smooth trail of clay preserved in the frigid shade where he had dragged the body.

His knees became weak. He collapsed into tears, sobbing, pounding his fist into the dirt.

"God, fucking, damn it!"

He went to the edge of the water and took out the pocket knife. He stared at the sharpest-looking blade, the saw blade, and realized he'd need both his wrists for his attempt to work. He began to rip off the bandages around his wounded hand, tossing the white gauze into the river. The strips flowed with the current as he struggled his hand free. He could feel the cold air on what was left of his right hand. He stared at the thin, alien claw still covered in stitches. The pinky and ring finger were clearly gone along with two thirds of his palm. He still had a thumb and an index finger and most of his middle: the top portion with his finger nail had been surgically removed. His middle and index were now close to the same size. More of his palm had been taken than he thought had been destroyed by the rifle. A 'C' shape had been carved into it, making his wrist appear enormous.

He submerged his hands into the rushing water to numb his wrists. The blood wouldn't flow as freely until his wrists were warm again, but he was aiming to curtail some of the pain as the pocket knife saw cut into his veins.

He had never heard of anyone back in Ohio doing it with a razor in the bathtub. That seemed like a luxurious, almost upper-class method like taking pills. In middle America, suicide was a gun's job.

He pulled his hands from the water and took the pocket knife. The blade shook in his mangled right hand. He exhaled, deeply, pursing his lips. Slowly, he dug the teeth of serrated steel into his left wrist. Bright red blood trickled over the saw. It stung worse than anything he had ever felt before.

"It's not across the road. It's up the street," a hoarse voice said.

He let go of the pocket knife and turned his head to see the figure standing with its knees in the shallow end of the river. The figure's eyes partially bulged from their sockets. A blackened hematoma had built up near its brow and the hands were pruned and wrinkled like skin stretched over bone. Most of the clothes were torn or missing from the rocks and current except for pieces of the jeans and the familiar black sweatshirt, though the band insignia had vanished. Its bloated skin had developed a viscous adipocere. It plucked the broken apple knife from his ear.

Rayne could hear the crunch as the blade came loose.

The dead kid's waterlogged face managed a smile as he stared at the gray viscera on the edge of the broken knife.

"Can't you do anything, right?"

"I killed you, Golem."

"That's not my name!" the animated corpse said. His teeth looked like bits of dried corn in darkened, purple gums.

"What was your real name then, Golem?"

He lunged forward, grabbing Rayne's throat with supernatural speed as if he had flown directly above the water. The cold, brittle hands squeezed, cutting off his airflow. Rayne could feel the bones loose within the dead skin. He fought to pull back the fingers, but it was like separating roots from centuries old stone. His face turned red. Unable to take in a breath, he reached up with his wounded hand and reverted to his old tactics and plucked at the swollen eyelid. As the corpse took the pressure off of his throat, pulling upward from the pain, Rayne's fingers held onto the cold sliver of flesh, peeling the eyelid and portion of his cheek away from his face. The glazed eye sagged within the colorless muscle in the exposed socket.

Rayne acted quick as he coughed, fighting to fill his lungs with air. He extended the knife blade of the multitool and plunged the tip into Golem's distended stomach. The gaseous stench of rotted organs emanated from the bloodless gash. He stabbed him again and ripped the knife to the left. Half-saponified intestines dropped from the torn stomach along with the carcass of a drowned river rat.

Golem looked at Rayne then at the rat and smiled again.

"Whoops," he said, taking a length of the waxy intestines and biting it in half to free himself of the coiled mess at his feet.

The dead kid's exposed eye glanced at Rayne's stolen pack.

"Got yourself a new one. Must have money, huh, traveler?"

"Don't you dare touch my shit again, you ugly fuck."

Golem lunged forward, his feet gliding over the dirt.

Rayne dove headlong toward the blackened drum.

He charged Rayne again, sweeping up the hill.

Rayne wrapped his right fingers around the neck of an intact 40oz bottle. He swung it like a club and hit the kid without shattering it. The kid's jaw sagged and some loose teeth spilled from his mouth. Rayne moved in for another strike, but Golem was quick. He stopped the bottle and crushed it with his skeletal hand. Rayne shielded himself from the shattered glass. He fell to his back and began kicking. Golem took hold of his legs and dragged him toward the river.

"I'll show you where I've been staying," he said. "I bet you'll like it."

He had the impossible strength to pull Rayne below in an instant, but, sadistically, he pulled him in as slow as he could. Rayne dug his fingers into the tough clay as Golem dragged him toward the river. Dirt and grime were getting inside the fresh cut on his wrist. The stitches on his wounded hand loosened from his straining. He screamed for help, but he was alone. There was no one working the construction site beyond the bridge. He let go of the dirt and began to writhe from side to side. Confused, Golem stopped dragging him and struggled against his legs.

Rayne pulled in his knees to get the kid's face closer to his own. He reached up with both hands, anchored his fingers to the dead kid's ears, and pressed his thumbs into his eyes. He forced his nails through the corneas and retinas until he could feel the cold vitreous fluid up to his knuckles. He pulled them out of the sockets and sprung his feet forward, launching the kid into the air.

The blinded corpse fell hard on the edge of the water and barely moved as Rayne approached. He took hold of his head and jerked it loose from his body. The joints and ligaments melted away as he tore through the neck. He stared at the severed head in his hands in silence when the mouth opened and sank its teeth into his stitch-covered palm. Using the rest of his strength, he pulled open the jaw, separating it from the rest of his skull, then tossed it into the river. It splashed and sank into the current. He took his time kicking the rest of the body into the water.

Taking his pack, he followed the river to a thicket of cattails. There, he pulled up some of the stalks and peeled away at their layers until he had a palmful of translucent jelly. He rubbed it into his stitches and his wrist. He had learned the trick in Oregon. You could also use honey if lifting a bottle of cortisone from a drug store was too difficult. He collapsed in the grass and waited for nightfall.

22

Desperation and the possibility of death, though he had just attempted suicide, drove him back to the center of Last Junction. It occurred to him only there that no little town square in the mountains ever had a twenty-four hour clinic. He'd have been lucky enough to find a drugstore. He ended up finding a gas station. There was no one behind the register. Rather than wait and break his hundred, he swiped a pack of bandaids and a tube of antibacterial ointment. He kept looking back, but no one ever showed up behind the counter to run him off.

He searched for a secluded place to work on himself and found a brick vestibule in a garden between two municipal buildings. He rubbed in half the tube and set the bandaids when his skin was dry. He could have died at any moment after the fight, and yet here he was taking measures against infection. The shock of ending up where he started drove him into a panic he could feel dilating his veins, inflaming his gut. But winning the fight a second time reminded him that he had enough grit to get out again. Despite being hurt and still sick with the memory of the reeking corpse, he had been gifted an unprecedented closure.

He followed the sidewalk under the street lamps. He was hungry. It had been more than a day since he ate his can of corned beef. He couldn't stop thinking about the eggs and sausages the religious couple had shared with him. The sidewalk ended and broke into a wide boulevard, opposite the road stood an old-timey luncheon stop: The Railroad Café.

Fuck it.

He pushed open the glass door. The bell affixed to the ceiling rang. The diner was lined with cracked red leather booths. The silver countertop was high, as were the stools. An old Latin man in pressed khakis, a white cotton shirt, and a black apron extinguished a cigarette on a coffee saucer as Rayne walked inside. There were two other people in the diner: a black man wearing maroon-tinted sunglasses and a fedora who kept a guitar case propped against his booth, and beside him sat the sheriff of Last Junction. Rayne recognized her green eyes. She had her uniform unbuttoned to reveal a gray sports bra. Her belt sagged on her hip. She held a raw steak against a gash on the side of her head. Her lip was swollen.

"Sorry, kid. We're sort of closed," the man behind the counter said.

Rayne slammed the hundred dollar bill on the stainless steel as he took a seat beside the sheriff.

"Then sort of open back up."

He paused and stared at Rayne for a moment. He saw through the faux bravado and looked deep into the desperation on his face. He looked at his half-hand.

"You're not like the rest of them are you?"

"It doesn't affect me. I wasn't born here."

"None of us were," he said, taking out a cup and saucer from the gray plastic wash rack. He set the cup in front of Rayne and, ignoring the money, filled it with hot black coffee.

"Put that away," he said. "Immigrants eat free."

He crumpled the hundred and set it back in his pocket.

"What about Native people? Aren't the settlers' descendants the actual immigrants?"

The sheriff spoke up as she placed a cigarette in the side of her mouth. "No, they were invaders. An immigrant's hands are only holding clothes, shoes, daily necessities, sometimes nothing. An invader's hands arrive clasping a gun and a scroll of new laws."

"I was really just asking about a guy you might know," Rayne said.

"It's a small town, kid. Everybody knows everybody. You talking about Jesse Christie?"

"Yeah."

"He doesn't come down here."

Rayne sipped his coffee.

"You look like hell, kid," the sheriff said.

"I just killed a boy for the second time," he said.

"You're hand wasn't like that when I first picked you up."

"No, it wasn't. Who tuned you up?"

"Former deputy. Had trouble taking orders from a black woman."

"You kill him?"

"It's all you can do when this season rolls around."

"Why do you stay the sheriff of this here town if it's cursed?"

"And let some white guy run the place?"

"Good point."

Rayne took another sip of the coffee. He looked up at the cafe owner.

"Where are you from?"

"Nicaragua. I'm Manuel. This is my café."

He turned to the sheriff.

"Your folks are from the Caribbean, right?"

She nodded, "Portsmouth, Dominica."

Rayne turned to the man in the booth. The man with the maroon sunglasses had taken out a Randall knife with a deer bone handle, carving flakes of wood from a small figurine of an elephant.

"Don't bother him," the sheriff said before Rayne could say anything. "That's Dr. Legs. He'll talk to you if he wants to."

"Can I have a cigarette?"

"How old are you?"

He exhaled, "I don't remember. I think I'm close to eighteen, but I'm not sure."

She tossed him a cigarette and a lighter.

He looked at the metal lighter for a moment before lighting the cigarette.

"Where are you from?" Manuel said.

"The Faroes," the sheriff said, answering before Rayne could. "He's out to see the world like the other lost street kids that come through here. Except something is different about this one. You're not like the other punks, are you?"

"I bleed like them," he said, showing off his hand.

Rayne smoked in silence. He ashed on the side of the saucer since no trays had been laid out. A prominent 'no smoking' sign hung on the glass door behind him.

Dr. Legs finished carving the elephant and stood it in the center of his table. Its ears were flat and the tusks short.

Manuel walked into the kitchen and returned with a bowl of chili.

"Don't tell me you're a vegetarian."

"Not a chance," Rayne said, stamping out the cigarette for later.

Manuel handed him a heavy metal spoon.

He stuck it into the fatty meat and beans. The spoon stood up on its own. He blew on a steaming portion before taking a bite and kept his mouth open as it sat on the edge of his tongue, trying to cool it with his breath. It burned him as he swallowed.

"It's hot. Be careful."

"Yeah, have you got any water?"

Manuel poured him a glass of ice water in a red plastic cup. The ice was crushed into small, easy-melting pebbles. "Coffee and beef," he said. "That's a man's dinner."

Rayne said nothing and kept on eating. He felt the need to thank them but his instincts told him to stay quiet, not to be ungrateful or rude but to remain stoic. As the chili cooled, he could taste the different spices: cinnamon, cumin, coriander, hot peppers. There were notes of things he didn't recognize. It had been a long time since he could remember eating anything properly spiced.

He kept trying to study Dr. Legs. It was difficult for Rayne to spy on him from across the room without attracting attention. With the sunglasses, the man's eyes were everywhere and on him all at once.

"Boy… why you looking at me like this?"

"Answer him," the sheriff said.

"I guess I'm wondering what you're doing carving that elephant."

"You were not looking at my elephant, nor on my guitar, dear boy. You wear looking at me. Trying to find my eyes. Well, here they are now for you to see."

Dr. Legs took off the shades with his spidery, wrinkled hand. Rayne noticed the cufflinks on his shirt were also carved from wood: two brown skulls. His eyes looked normal, dark. He had crows feet in the corners of his old face like cross hatches on a sketch.

"Tell me, what do you see in them?" he said.

"I don't know."

"Neither do I," he said. "You are drowning."

"Am I?"

"You are. You left the safety of the harbor, but the ocean is bigger than you thought."

"I feel more like I was born at sea."

His remark made the old man laugh. "Very well. Very astute," he said. "But very wrong."

"I'm always wrong," he said.

Rayne tried to eat his chili as fast as he could. He wanted to get out of this diner. He also wanted to ask the sheriff for another ride back to the county line. He kept quiet, waiting for the right time to ask.

"Where are you from, Mr. Legs?"

The room went silent.

Rayne continued.

"Well, just… in keeping with the nautical theme here, I wondered if you were from the Caribbean as with our sheriff."

Manuel leaned over Rayne.

"Dr. Legs is a Shona *nganga* from Zimbabwe," he whispered.

"What exactly does that mean?"

Manuel didn't answer. He smiled and stepped away.

Rayne finished his chili and turned to Dr. Legs.

"What are you?"

Dr. Legs scowled at him.

"He's an African witch doctor," the sheriff said.

Rayne nodded. "Ah, hah," he said, setting the unfinished cigarette in his outside pocket. "That is interesting."

"Watch it, kid."

Rayne swigged the remainder of his coffee. He stood up as if he were about to leave.

"Thank you very much for the hospitality."

None of them replied.

He looked at the sheriff. Her eyes didn't meet his, they remained dead set on Manuel who had stepped into the corner beyond the cash register to turn on a small portable radio. It was old, the quality of the sound significantly diminished. The black box, half of which was taken up by the single massive speaker, sat on a shelf used to store cleaning supplies beside the spent glass tube of a Mexican candle, its rim blackened. Rayne wasn't expecting to hear Country music, and, least of all, a song he happened to recognize. Dorn had played Country incessantly in the house. Rayne's Punk Rock collection started as a measure against the high-lonesome drawl of Waylon Jennings.

Willy your wild as the blue Texas northern, the song played, crystalized in static.

Manuel fixed himself a glass of ice water and drank, staring at the radio as if it were about to explode.

Rayne walked up to the window glass and looked at the town at night. A gust of frigid wind stirred the street lights. He looked back at the three of them. The sheriff had changed the position of the steak on her bruised face. He thought about being dropped off at the church. Maybe he would say something snarky or sacrilegious to her, but could think of nothing and walked out the door.

23

Rayne pulled himself up with his good hand and crested the hill where the concrete steps overlooked a public garden. Resting himself on the cold iron rail, he observed the cast-bronze plaques and canned lights hidden within the shrubs. The magnolias shuddered in the wind. This place, he imagined, must be crawling with traveling kids in the summer. The trash bins were full of cheap beer cans and he saw a few tags on the edge of the public restroom door. He tried to get inside for the night but the door was sealed by a hefty deadbolt.

Beyond the garden, where the terrain leveled out, he could see a row of houses each one dilapidated and forgotten leading up to a towering school building equally derelict in appearance. It was an unusual place for the bad part of town. He noticed this kind of setup more often in the Southeast than anywhere else he had traveled. The roads here were planned without a grid, the buildings shared little uniformity, and the affluent often squeezed themselves close to the destitute as if to taunt them. Two ends of the same street could be an entire universe of existence away from one another as though two cities had been stitched together.

He crouched beneath the rail and slid down the opposite end of the hill. His boots pulled up chunks of soil and smears of green. He trekked through the shrubs and topiaries, kicking over a few of the plastic canned lights as he raced to the edge of the sidewalk. He checked both sides of the street and crossed into the row of abandoned housing. There were small two-level houses crammed into each plot on either side of the narrow way, sometimes only a foot of space between them where only weeds grew and the plastic cases of the energy meters reached out to scrape the vinyl siding of the next house. Some had small patios decorated in melted candles, broken porch swings, overflowing cigarette stubs like masses of dead insects, and piles black garbage bags. Most had waist-high iron gates sectioning off the overgrown yards. He continued down the cracked sidewalk. Everything went dark. The streetlamps' reach ended and his eyes were slow to adjust. The insides of the homes were opaque caverns. He stopped at the elementary school and sat on the steps.

Headlights and the sound of a loud engine approached from his left on the narrow road. He huddled against the brick pillar and watched as the familiar white van hurtled toward the school. The van swerved, its lights capturing everything around him. He lowered his head trying to stay hidden.

The breaks screeched.

He didn't look to see who was driving.

The van sat there, the engine humming. It was as if it could sense him.

He considered making a break for it, running passed the lights and disappearing into the shadows. He got ready to sprint. He lifted up his head and stopped.

It was Jac.

She lowered the passenger window.

"Rayne?"

He kept his distance .

"Jac," he said.

"I thought you were dead," she said. "I couldn't find you at the hospital."

"I got out."

He took out the multitool and flicked open the blade behind his back.

"How's your hand?"

He switched hands with the tool and showed her his bandaged, stitched, fingers and remaining palm.

"Do you want a ride?" she said.

"Depends on where you're going."

Neither of them spoke.

Even from a distance, Rayne could see Jac's face had changed. She had lost color. Her right eyelid was bruised. Her cheeks were gaunt.

He took a few steps toward the van.

"Where *are* you going, Jac?"

She coughed before she spoke. Her voice sounded deeper.

"Anywhere but here."

He paused.

"I'm going now, so if you wanna come with me you've got to make up your mind."

"Open up the side door," he said.

"It's unlocked. You can open it up on your own."

Clenching the blade, he crept toward the door handle and extended his wounded hand. He flicked open the lock and let the momentum slowly open up the back on its own. The rollers squeaked as the door glided along the inner track to reveal nothing but empty seats.

"Hit the lights," he said.

She obliged without comment.

Still nothing.

No bags. No doll.

He looked at Jac and saw she had a gut wound. There was a circular stain of semi-congealed blood and a small hole in her brown overalls. In her hands, she clutched Cain's Beretta 9mm.

"What's that for?"

"*You*, in case you try anything," she said.

He closed the side door and got inside from the passenger's seat. He set his pack between his legs.

She killed the cabin lights and drove.

24

He could see abandoned houses for miles. Roof shingles littered the grass in the small lawns along with broken porcelain and paper bags. A few of the squat homes had caved in completely. Unlike other discarded lots he had seen across the country, whether he was riding a double stack through an aborted housing project or defunct textile mill, he could always read the graffiti. Any kind of mural or gang tag was absent from the peeling walls here.

Jac was driving with one hand. The other gripped the 9mm, her finger looped inside the trigger guard.

"You shouldn't hold the gun like that when you're driving," he said.

She smiled. It was a grim, jaded smile. She raised her lip just enough that he could see the blood congealing in between her teeth. She had been coughing blood. He looked at her wound. It was still fresh. She hadn't sustained the injury at the hospital.

"Where were you born?" he said.

"What?"

"Are your parents American?"

"What the fuck are you asking me that for?"

"Forget it," he said. "But please, set the gun down. I'm not going to grab it. As far as I'm concerned it's yours. It belongs to you."

She reluctantly set the pistol, muzzle down, in the cup holder.

He took out his cigarette from the diner and his matches to occupy his hands.

"It's not mine, though," she said, hands at two and ten on the wheel.

"I know," he said, blowing smoke. "How hurt are you?"

"It's not as bad as it looks."

They drove past an old man standing on the edge of the road in a white nightgown. He was limping. Jac pressed down on the gas and sped past him. The rows of houses ended and blackened woods cropped up around them. She slowed the Chevy in order to handle the turns. They were driving on the mountain roads now, the same roads where he had encountered the hunter.

"As soon as we find a place to stop, I need to take a hit."

"I don't think we should stop," he said, passing her the Camel.

She took a quick drag on the cigarette and passed it back.

"I need the energy to drive all night. I don't want to stop till we're in Miami, Florida. Get the fuck out of the cold."

"Real close to Canada, huh?"

She looked at him briefly.

"I'm the one driving the van. I get to say where we're going."

"I'll give you a hundred dollars to take us to Niagara Falls."

He showed her the money.

"Alright, north it is."

There was a lookout point at the top of the mountain. She pulled off into the gravel.

"Make it quick," he said.

She killed the engine and rifled through a small canvas bag at her feet. Her straight shooter was gone. In its place, she had constructed a small rig from a lightbulb and a plastic tube. The hit was loaded and ready to go. She flicked the lighter and started rocking the bulb from side to side under the butane flame. She inhaled through the straw and exhaled a white, vinegar-smelling cloud. He rolled down his window to let the lingering smoke disperse. He passed her the cigarette again, like a chaser. She took a short drag, handed it back, and produced another massive plume of meth smoke. He rolled the window down all the way, and finished off the cigarette trying to keep himself from getting a contact high. When the cloud was gone, he took one last drag off the filter and tossed the ember out of the car. Jac turned the key and pressed down on the gas.

"Make sure my shit isn't broken," she said.

Rayne leaned over to make sure her impromptu pipe was safe inside her bag.

"What happened to the other one?"

She smiled. It was genuine this time. "It cracked after I did a hot rail."

He nodded as he rolled up the window.

"Just don't get us killed."

Her face changed.

"You're pretty fuckin' judgmental for a traveler. And pretty fuckin' ungrateful for someone who's getting a ride all the way to Niagara Falls. A hundred bucks doesn't make you a goddamned martyr, you know. You got a problem that I use? Because if I didn't, I'd fall asleep and we... we'd be dead then. So... watch it man."

"No judgement," he said. "Just keep an eye on the road, these are tough turns."

"Oh, because a woman can't fuckin' drive?"

"That's not what I said."

"Well, what the fuck are you saying?"

He kept quiet. She slowed the van around another winding turn, then burst into tears.

"I'm sorry," she said. "It's been a traumatic few days is all. That's my fault."

"Don't worry about it."

"I've seen so many horrible things, Rayne. Things I can't explain."

"Me too," he said, keeping his attention on the road.

She went silent for the next half mile, then broke into laughter. He listened to her laugh for a while. When she finally stopped, he rested his head back and attempted to relax and savor the quiet. It didn't last.

"He's following us!" she said, in a sudden panic. "That's him."

Rayne sat up and saw Jac staring into the rearview mirror. He looked into his own mirror and could make out a black SUV following them.

"A lot of people have cars like that. It could be anybody."

"No," she said, frantically shaking her head. "I know it's him. He said he wouldn't let me leave."

She gunned the engine as they descended the northern slope of the big mountain. This stretch of the woods was Jesse's territory, close to the party cabin. It made sense that Cain would find them here. Jac was right. Rayne glanced back at the black SUV as it sped up behind them. All along, it had probably been Cain who had taken his poncho on that lonely road outside town. The man had a room in the house where he stashed stolen backpacks for God's sake. He thought about Cain and he thought about the doll, the lumberjack that kept haunting him. He was afraid but his adrenaline wasn't flowing. He was steady. Perhaps his body had used all of it like an ecstasy fiend the day after, but how was he supposed to know how the human adrenal gland worked?

"Besides the gun, what else did you take from him?"

"Two-hundred dollars and some weed."

"Good," he said. "We'll need more than a hundred to get to Niagara."

"We're not going to make it to Niagara, you idiot. There's gonna be a manhunt and a police blockade by the time we're in Tennessee."

"No one but Cain is going to be looking for us," he said. "Remember when you said you saw things you couldn't explain?"

She nodded.

"Trust me, we're gonna be just fine as long as we stay on the road and get out of this place."

He half-believed himself.

The SUV tailed them by less than a foot and shined its brights into their mirrors.

"He's not gonna let me go. He's done things to me."

Rayne unbuckled his seatbelt and grabbed the pistol.

"Keep driving," he said. "If I fall out, keep going. Throw my pack on the side of the road. I'll find it if I'm alive." He crawled across the seats to the back of the van.

"What are you doing?"

"Keep driving."

He found his footing and kept his spine pressed against the final row of seats, positioning himself to fall backward when he lost balance. He pulled the handle on the left tailgate door. It didn't budge.

"Unlock the backdoors."

She searched the dashboard and her armrest.

"I don't see anything. I don't think it opens when you're driving."

He aimed to shoot the lock, but saw a small nodule of plastic close to the handle. He pushed it in and pulled the handle again. The door swung open and immediately slammed shut from the momentum. He opened it halfway and propped it ajar with his foot. He extended his arm and fired the pistol with his wounded hand. A bullet wrinkled the hood. Two more shots burst the tinted windshield. He could almost see Cain past the exposed velvet black dash at the edge of the wheel. Cain accelerated and crashed into the back of the Chevy. Rayne held onto the back-seat. He lined up another shot. The SUV's grill was destroyed, latticed with streaks of white paint. Jac continued without swerving. She was drenched in sweat.

"Hold on!"

Rayne gripped the synthetic vinyl even tighter. His feet lifted off the floor as she took a hard left onto the dirt road hidden in the brush. The van rocked from side to side on the rough terrain. The tailgate door swung open. Cain was following them on the same backroad.

"I don't think the shortcut was worth it," he said.

"It's not a shortcut."

"Then what the fuck are you doing?"

She didn't answer.

The world upended. Rayne's body was pinned to the ceiling, then thrashed against the seats. The Chevy had stopped dead. The gun had slipped from his hand. He stood in the lopsided cabin and forced open the side door. Crawling into the grass, he followed the tire impressions where the van had veered off the dirt. He pried open the passenger door and took his pack. Jac had vanished. The steering wheel and the windshield were also gone. There were a few jagged pieces of glass along the frame close to what was left of the engine: a mass of intricate tubes and warped bands of hot steel wrapped around a large, moss-encrusted boulder. Smoke and steam billowed upward in the last remaining headlight's dying glow.

He dove behind a tree as Cain drove up to the wreckage. The SUV stalled as the old man cranked the emergency break and left the engine running before he stepped out into the wild grass. His face looked different. He was wearing glasses. Rayne didn't remember having seen him with glasses. The angular frames made his face smaller, and wasn't certain, at least not at first, that he was looking at the same sinister, retiree. His stringy gray hair had also been smoothed back by a moist handful of product, which glistened even more than usual mixed in with his cold sweat, and wrangled into a ponytail by a rubber band. He gazed at the Chevy long enough that Rayne thought he could see him behind the tree, but the darkness was on his side. The SUV's headlights were aimed at the totaled, white van and the greater woodland beyond the outcropping of boulders. The light glanced off the slick lichen-patched trunks and ethereal shrubs parceled across the forest floor. There was no sign of Jac's body.

Rayne crouched behind the bulk of the tree hidden in shadow. His breaths were silent. He tried to imagine Jac's body being flung from the driver's seat. How far could she have flown through the air before hitting a tree or a rock, before snapping her neck or her spine? It would be a miracle if she were alive out there in the dirt, lying cold and bloody, her face covered in glass.

Cain returned to his idled vehicle and opened the door to the backseat. He took out a .22 caliber rifle and a Coleman lantern. He pumped the bottom portion of the pressure lamp, then took out a lighter to ignite the mantle. He carried it across the rocks and into the woods with him. He held the butt of the rifle awkwardly in the crook of his free shoulder. The light surrounded him, moving with him like an aura, illuminating the sides of the trees as he moved.

Rayne watched as the light moved further into the dark. He stood up from behind the tree and ran toward the black SUV. He opened the driver's side door, and reached inside to cut the engine and the lights. That would get his attention. He threw the keys as far as he could into the bushes, then crept toward the smoldering van. He took out the canvas bag and began to search through her things. He could barely see. The lightbulb she had been smoking from had shattered. There were a few crumpled bills inside and he stashed them in his pockets. There was no use wasting money if Jac was already dead. He didn't bother looking through the van to find the 9mm. It was probably lying somewhere hidden in the grass. Instead, he retreated to Cain's vehicle once again and searched the center console for another weapon. He found a wood-handled, snub-nosed revolver. It was more cumbersome to grip with his remaining fingers than the Beretta. He struggled against the thick metal before discovering the mechanism to release the cylinder. It was loaded. The bottoms of the cartridges looked like foreign currency with the primercaps intact. He snapped the cylinder back into the frame of the gun and pulled back the hammer. Crouched low, he inched toward the boulders waiting for the light to return.

Cain trampled back through the brush still carrying the camping lantern in front of him, resting the barrel of the rifle on his extended forearm to level his shot. The light was his biggest mistake. With it, Rayne knew exactly where to shoot. He raised the pistol over the rock and fired twice. The flash lit up his face.

The second shot had been a mistake but proved to be effective. Cain had dropped the lantern into the brush.

Rayne could only see the soles of his boots twitching, kicking up dirt as he screamed in pain. He waited, listening to him sobbing and screaming, for a barrage of retaliating fire, but it never came. He crawled over the boulders and approached him, rolling the lantern closer along the ground with the edge of his foot. Cain was hit in the shoulder and the side of his stomach. The blood was soaking through his clothes. The rifle was just out of his reach. Rayne set the gun in his coat pocket and picked up the semi-automatic rifle.

"Did you see Jac?"

Cain yelled at him without saying anything.

"I'd say I don't think anybody could survive a crash like that, but I did."

Cain pressed his hands against his gut wound to stop the bleeding and let out a shrill, animalistic screech.

"I can't take either one of the cars. I'm always right back where I started in this fuckin' place. At least, I'm not you right now. At least I can still walk away," he said, aiming the barrel a few inches from Cain's crotch. "Have you killed any kids?"

Cain raised his bloody hands in a feeble attempt to shield himself.

"I feel like this town is half-alive. Like it shows me things. It keeps showing me a little doll and a bunch of chopped-up kids in plastic bags. Does that mean anything?"

Cain continued to sob as a thin streak of blood dribbled down his chin.

Rayne pressed the barrel of the rifle against the zipper of the old man's jeans and fired four times. Blood welled up in the hefty blue fabric and poured out between his legs. His screams only grew louder as he writhed from side to side in the dirt. Rayne lifted the rifle and shot his throat to stifle the screams. Once Cain was quiet, he thrust the rifle like a javelin into the brush and picked up the lantern, leaving him to bleed out as he made his way back to the road.

25

A quiet sedan rolled up behind him on one of the difficult turns; the kind that stretched around the flat surfaces of the rocks at the edge of the mountain and left no space for error where the foliage ended and, at night, the stars were revealed, brighter even in the heavy bucolic dark. The car turned the corner and vanished past the rocks like a ghost. He heard nothing, no engine grind, no tailpipe rattle. Around the bend, the sedan had stopped and the driver's window rolled down. He held onto the pistol in his coat pocket and kept his distance, but the driver leaned out of the open window.

"Need a ride?"

Rayne lifted the lantern.

The driver looked to be in his mid-forties. His receding black hair was peppered with streaks of gray. His hands were empty. Rayne stepped closer.

"Is that an electric car?"

"Yeah, it's an old Nissan Leaf."

He thought it was strange to call it old. It was a brand new electric car as far as he could tell. He figured the guy was rich.

"Where are you headed?"

"North," he said.

"Can you get me to Tennessee?"

"How's Knoxville sound?"

Rayne gripped the pistol in his pocket and kept the lantern raised with his intact hand.

"I just need to get to the state line, really."

"That's not far at all. I can take you there."

"Alright."

"Just one thing."

"Yeah?"

"You gotta turn that fire hazard you're holding off. You ever seen one of those old Coleman's go up in flames. I'm not having that in my car."

"Fair enough," Rayne said. He didn't like the lantern either. It was cumbersome and the heat was beginning to singe his hand. He released the pressure and turned off the light, discarding it along the road as he approached the car.

"You're just gonna leave it?" the stranger said.

"I don't need it."

The stranger moved the passenger's seat back to give Rayne's backpack room which he set between his legs before buckling the seatbelt. The car had a clean interior and smelled of coffee. The stranger shut off the overhead dash lights and drove down the road.

"You just passing through?" Rayne said.

"Actually, I was trying to avoid this area and go around, but I missed an exit and my GPS kind of sucked me back this way."

"This place has a way of doing that. First time?"

"Unfortunately, no. I got lost here a long time ago. Not a fan of Appalachia in general."

Rayne kept his eyes on the stranger's hands, made sure they stayed two and ten on the wheel when he wasn't swilling the coffee he kept in the side console. He had a tall thermos of coffee with a retractable cap that he flicked open with his thumb whenever he took a drink.

"You pulling an all-nighter?"

"Sort of. Trying to make it to Knoxville... at least by tonight."

They passed a small, green municipal sign: ANDREW JACKSON COUNTY LINE. He wasn't at ease. He would kill the driver and take the car if he tried anything.

"How come your GPS isn't on?"

"I don't trust it until around back roads. I usually flip it on once I'm back on the interstate."

"No offense, but that seems pretty counterintuitive," Rayne said.

"It does when you say it out loud like that, but, trust me, if I turned it on now all it would do is bring around in circles."

"You're sure you know where you're going?"

"I know Tennessee is this way. We're almost out of the woods," the stranger said.

"Possibly."

"What makes you so unsure?"

"I made it all the way to the Smoky Mountains just a few days ago, then I hopped a freight train and it sent me right back where I started."

"Well..." the stranger said before gathering his thoughts. "I don't plan on making a quick turnaround anytime tonight. I'm gonna make it to Knoxville even if the tires fall out of my wheel wells."

Rayne kept watching his hands. He held the steering wheel odd. It was the way he kept his pinky extended.

"You got kids?"

"Nope. No kids."

"You single?"

"I'm married."

"Can you not have kids?"

"We could if we wanted to."

"You just don't?"

"We don't."

"I'm sure your wife has feelings."

"About havings kids? No. She doesn't secretly want kids."

"All women, on some level, want to have kids."

"You're still young," the stranger said. smiling. "You don't know everything yet. Life surprises you."

Rayne coughed and adjusted his feet.

"Why did you pick me up?"

"You looked like you needed help."

"Do you typically pick up hitchhikers?"

"Hitchhikers? No. You weren't thumbing a ride. It looked like you were screwed and needed help. Like your car might have been broken down, or something went wrong at your campsite."

"You a Christian?"

The stranger shook his head.

"Atheist?"

"I don't believe in God."

"So you're an atheist?"

"Hard to say. Maybe I believe in more than one god."

"That's a really weird thing to say, dude. I only asked because the last decent folks I met around here were ministers or something."

"You ask an awful lot of questions. You always chat up strangers on the road?"

Rayne paused. "Actually, no. I guess I'm just used to everyone constantly checking me out, asking me what I'm doing and where the fuck I come from."

"I don't need to know where you're from."

Rayne stared at the night out the window, still keeping an eye on the driver in the dark reflection. He looked around the car, then turned to check the backseat. He was expecting to see the doll staring back at him, but all he could make out was a suitcase and paperback book. The pages were warped and frayed. The cover was nearly peeled off. He looked back at the driver.

"Can I see what you're reading?"

"Sure."

He reached out for the book and set in on the top of his pack. It was a copy of *Desolation Angels* by Jack Kerouac. With his good hand, he skipped through the introduction and the first few pages and landed on the second chapter. He squinted to see one sentence in the break between the shadows.

"When I get to the top of Desolation Peak and everybody leaves on mules and I'm all alone I will come face to face with God or Tathagata and find out once and for all what is the meaning of all this existence and suffering and going to and fro in vain" but instead I'd come face to face with myself

The rest of the run-on sentence was hidden in the darkness and all he could make out after, toward the bottom of the page were the words "or jump off the mountain."

"This was my mom's favorite book," he said.

"Sad book."

"She talked about it like it was this great adventure, this kind of magical truth. We didn't have a Bible in the house. This was our Bible."

"The real Jack Kerouac would have hated that."

"He hated his own books?"

"No, he was a devoted Catholic."

"I thought he was Buddhist?"

"Not really. Buddhism was just the flavor of the day back then. No, Kerouac had a portrait of the Pope in his house."

"What are you some kind of scholar?"

"No, I just watched a documentary about it on TV once."

Rayne smirked and kept sifting through the pages. The stranger took another swig of coffee from the tall thermos.

"I noticed you only use your left hand. The other one's been stuck in your pocket this whole time. You got a gun?"

Rayne closed the book.

"Yeah, I do. Why? Do you want to see it?"

"No, not really. Just don't shoot me."

"I'm not like that, man. I'm not a wacko. I just have to stay protected."

"I get it. I gotta protect myself too."

Rayne sat in silence for the next mile. His hand was sweaty in the pocket. He wanted to scratch it but he wasn't prepared to let his guard down.

"This copy even looks a lot like my mom's," he finally said to break the quiet.

"It is," the stranger said.

"What are you fuckin' saying?"

"That's mom's copy of *Desolation Angels*."

The stranger didn't speak for a moment and let his shoulders drop as he drove. He wasn't afraid of Rayne's gun.

"When I went back to Ohio, they gave me a few of Dorn's things he left behind, some baseball memorabilia, a bottle of expensive Pappy Van Winkle with half a finger left in it, just garbage I immediately threw out, but... he still had her copy of the book."

Rayne winced and took out the pistol.

The stranger didn't react.

"She had a Danish copy--probably because there wasn't a Faroese version at the time--that she brought with her to Canada when we first left the islands. It got lost though. Then she had this one. Remember when we used to look at the picture of Kerouac on the cover looking all cool with his jean jacket and smoking and we thought he might be our dad?"

Rayne pulled back the hammer on the pistol.

"I don't know how you know that, but if you continue I'll shoot. Are you some kind of demon?"

"I'm you, Dag. I'm you at 41-years-old."

"You look like you're fifty."

"Extra years of rough livin' can do that to you."

Rayne pointed the barrel of the gun at the glove compartment as he set the hammer back in place.

"Nice try," he said, reaching up to the dashboard light. "But if you were me, you'd have *this* wrong with you." He showed him his wounded hand.

The stranger held onto the steering wheel and casually bit the tip of his ring finger. He pulled at the skin and slipped out of the silicon sleeve which fit over his mangled hand like a glove. The false fingers were incredibly lifelike. Rayne pocketed the pistol.

"Son of a bitch. Nobody but mom ever called me, Dag."

"Except Dorn, but he'd say Dags."

"I got so sick it."

"Yeah, he was real piece of shit."

"How did you get here?"

"I don't know. I got lost and then I ended up back here after all these years. Once I saw you, saw myself on the road, I remembered everything. I knew how far to go and what to do to get there, the same thing happened to me."

"Get where?"

He pointed through the windshield. Rayne looked ahead. The blue and white sign read: TENNESSEE THE VOLUNTEER STATE WELCOMES YOU.

"Oh, thank god."

"Piece of advice," Dagur said. "Don't hop any trains going south." He slowed the car and put it in park.

"What are you doing?"

"This is where you get out."

"Fuck that, take me all the way Virginia with you."

"That's what I said too. But this is where you'll drop me off eventually. I think we can only help each other for so many miles without messing something up. For some reason you and I get to cheat a little bit. Just enough to get a leg up."

"What happens to me after this?"

"Your whole life."

"Come on, man. Give me something."

"Get your hand looked at when you can."

Rayne grabbed his bag and stepped out of the car. He stood under the highway sign and watched the Nissan disintegrate into the dark.

26

The road had teeth, little fibrous fangs that gripped flesh and tore away at the muscles. He was a real traveler now with shards of the road stuck forever in his scarred tissue. He knew that the road had no truth to offer. Those seeking truth were bitten deeper than those who only sought a means. Dagur limped in the morning half-light toward the motel at the edge of the highway exit. Part of the way, as he had trekked in the dark through the night, his leg had begun to swell up--residual trauma from the crash in the Jac's Astro.

He had a lean three hundred dollars on him now and he needed shelter, shelter and rest. Limping toward the Free Eagle Inn, he took note of the beauty of the morning dew. He passed through the glass door. The bell rang. The girl behind the front desk and bullet-proof glass looked up, exhaustion apparent behind her faded black eyeshadow.

"How much for a night?"

"Fifty bucks a night," she said. "You have to have an I.D."

He gave her a hundred and the college I.D. of Paul De Bakker.

"I need a room for two nights," he said.

"Two nights?"

"Yeah."

"Did you just walk here."

"All the way from Last Junction," he said.

"From where?"

He took a room on the second floor with a chaotic rug pattern and a large television. The first thing he did was take a bath, submerging his swollen leg in the hot water. Dirt and grime from his skin rose up and pooled around the edge of the tub.

He watched *The Simpsons* on cable and laughed that night. He laughed as he spread himself across the bed remote in hand. He laughed like he hadn't in a long time.

The End